Country People

SOME *BORZOI* BOOKS
SPRING, 1924

THE PHILOSOPHER'S STONE
J. ANKER LARSEN

AN ISLAND CHRONICLE
WILLIAM CUMMINGS

WOMEN AND WIVES
HARVEY FERGUSSON

THE PITIFUL WIFE
STORM JAMESON

TONY
STEPHEN HUDSON

IMPERTURBE
ELLIOT H. PAUL

WINE OF FURY
LEIGH ROGERS

SANDOVAL
THOMAS BEER

Country People

Ruth Suckow

New York
Alfred · A · Knopf
1924

813.5 $S112e$

Recat. 9-20-54 cdn,

1483

Contents

PART ONE

I: August Kaetterhenry's Place   9
II: The Kaetterhenrys   14
III: Emma Stille   32

PART TWO

I: The Farm and the Children   53
II: Grandma and Grandpa   67
III: Loosening Up   82
IV: The War   100

PART THREE

I: Operation   115
II: Town   133

PART FOUR

I: Retired Farmers   151
II: Obituary   167
III: The Estate   185
IV: Mrs. Emma Kaetterhenry   199

Part One

I: *August Kaetterhenry's Place*

SOME of the best land in the country, people said, was right here in Richland Township. The soil in Wapsipinicon County was a little inclined to be sandy, didn't bring quite the price of the very best Iowa farming-land; but this stretch in here between Richland and "Wapsie" didn't give the farmers much chance for complaint.

This was the road that was later made a highway. It had a slight jog about a mile out of Richland. Tall cottonwoods grew on one side, on the other a tangle of bushes. There was always a kind of mud-hole here, sifted over with leaves and little fluffs from the cottonwoods; a bad place in the road, closed in and shaded.

Beyond this it was all straight going to "Wapsie." The land spread out rich and rolling, in smooth, tilted vistas of square fields, green, yellow, and earth-brown, trees growing in full-leaved clusters down about the banks of the

9

little caved-in creeks in the pastures or standing lone, and slanting, on the crests of the low, rounded hills. In the distance the groves of farms were softened, blurred together; the far-off rising land was swathed in blue, a faint milky tint in which dim figures of trees were swimming.

A pink frame school-house stood on one side of the road. The long grass was trampled this way and that by the children's feet. Over beyond Ed Angell's place lay the Grove, where Sunday-School picnics and Fourth of July celebrations were held—a rich, thick cluster of trees, oaks and hickories, spreading over the hill and down the depressions of the slope, dark green upon the paler green of the short-cropped grass on the hill-side. The road went high and straight until it dipped down into "Wapsie," which lay deep in trees, the red stone tower of the court-house rising out of thick tufts of elms.

The farms were good along this road. A good class of people had settled here, German and English most of them. Men who kept an eye out for land deals noted shrewdly how well the buildings and barbed-wire fences were kept up, the red barns and silos, the prim white houses, square or with an ell, some of them with front yards enclosed in fences, and rose or snowball bushes growing. Most of these farmers—except the LaRues, who lived in a dingy, unpainted house with a bare farm-yard and a hog-pen of trampled, sloughy mud—drove into town in neat "two-seated rigs" with good teams. The cattle feeding in the pastures that sloped down, emerald-green, turfy, almost mossy, to the edges of the creeks were sleek and brown.

Over on the cross-roads there were more woods, and it was hillier. The farm-buildings were poorer, the fences slacker. These were the farms where people from "Wapsie" drove out to buy cheap a chicken, a goose, or a few crates of berries.

The place on the north of the road, beyond LaRue's, was August Kaetterhenry's.

It was a neat, plain farm, two hundred and fifty acres, virtually all under cultivation. The house was set back at what was termed "a nice distance" from the road—a white house with pink trimmings and a narrow porch. The front yard was not fenced in, but August made the boys keep the grass mowed, and it presented a neat appearance. Tall summer lilies, orange with dark spots, grew near the front porch in a spread-

11

ing patch. On the west of the house stood the wind-break—two rows of elms that were lofty now, rather thin, and close together. The lawn ended at their trunks in a ridge of high grass and feathery weeds that the boys could not keep cut. A barbed-wire fence, caught together in one place by a wooden staple, separated them from the cornfield. The lofty upper branches rustled and moved slightly against the blue sky. In the evening their outlines were blurred and there was a sadness in their dark leafiness, high and motionless.

The wide yard sloped east to the barns and sheds across "the drive." It was worn bare of grass about the buildings and scattered with chicken fluff and droppings. The geese ran squawking across it when teams drove in. The great barn stood at the end of the slope, raised on a high foundation, with an inclined platform of heavy planks that thundered and shook under the horses' hoofs. Everyone about here remembered when August Kaetterhenry had put up this barn. It was painted white, as was the silo, and on the peak of the roof were two cupolas with slatted sides, and lightning-rods that glittered intermittently upon the blueness of the sky.

August Kaetterhenry's Place

On the side toward the road was painted in large black letters slowly getting weather-dimmed:

AUGUST KAETTERHENRY
1907

It was one of the best barns in the country there when it was put up. All of Kaetterhenry's buildings were good. The old barn had been made over by his brother-in-law, Hans Stille, into a granary and milk-house, painted white, too, the ground always slippery and muddy about the milk-house, a dribble of yellow ears leaking out from the corn-crib, kernels scattered in front of it, where the chickens were pecking. On the slope nearer the house the windmill stood, with the tank beside it, a bare steel skeleton giving off sudden flashes, the grey-painted wheel turning now fast, now slow, up there in the sky.

"Yes," people said when they drove past, "Kaetterhenry's done pretty good here. Well, he's a worker all right."

They admired the neat, square fields of oats and corn, the high, rolling pasture dotted with white clover, a few wild plum-trees set slanting, delicate and lonely, here and there.

"Yes, sir, he's got a nice farm."

II: *The Kaetterhenrys*

AUGUST KAETTERHENRY had not always had a farm like this. He had had to work for what he had got, like most of the people in that country. He hadn't got prosperous by wishing. There were plenty of people who could remember when he first came into the Richland neighbourhood. Along about the early eighties or late seventies it must have been, because he had worked for Henry Baumgartner, and it was in 1884 or "somewheres around" that the Baumgartners had moved into town. He came from Turkey Creek, where there were still "a whole raft of those Kaetterhenrys." August was one of old Casper Kaetterhenry's boys.

Turkey Creek was a little backwoods town about fifteen miles north of Richland, up in the timber. It still had no railroad and was "years behind the times," but some of the farmers around there had money, if they only cared to spend it. It was a good trading-centre. There

14

was a large German settlement around Turkey
Creek, more Germans than in the country near
Richland, which had a good many settlers from
Somerset, in England. Turkey Creek had had
Scotch and Yankee settlers in the first place, trap-
pers and woodsmen; but the Germans coming
in to farm had crowded these people out. They
were a slow, hard-headed set, those Turkey Creek
Germans, but they were better than the timber-
men, who had had, as old men who knew that
country liked to tell, "some pretty rough characters among them." The Germans were hard-
working, money-savers, and they had come to
make homes for themselves.

It was Henry Baumgartner who had brought
them there in the first place—old Henry Baumgartner. He was gone now, but he had been
"quite a character" in his day. He was a Prus-
sian who had come to this country when he was
only a boy. He was said to have worked at one
of the forges in Pennsylvania. There was a
story of how, when he had been working there,
he had been converted to German Methodism.
He had come out to Iowa in a very early day
and had bought up large tracts of timber-land
when it was selling for almost nothing. Later,

15

in the interests of both riches and religion, which the old man had always shrewdly worked together, he had sent back to Prussia and got a dozen families to come and settle on his land, promising them help in getting started on the condition that they should all become German Methodists. He had been afraid that the German Catholics, who had a settlement over in the hills at Holy Cross, would "get a hold" in the Turkey timber. That was the way that large German Methodist community had first started. Other Germans had begun coming in until the region was full of them. Most of them had been Lutherans in the old country, but Henry Baumgartner had been careful to see that there was no Lutheran church started here.

It was a hilly region, timber- and bottomland. The people had lived primitively there; many of them did still. There were still a few of the old log cabins to be seen in isolated places, down on the Turkey Bottom. In those early days they had all lived in log cabins. The old-timers could remember well when the first framehouse in the country had gone up on old Herman Klaus's farm. Turkey Creek had been a wild little timber town with a few wooden stores and houses, after the first old log buildings had gone down, and the town hall, of the native yellow limestone, that was standing yet at the end of the business street, and where now the community held the harvest-home supper and the young people had dances.

The Kaetterhenrys had lived in one of those log houses on the same land where one of them, a half-brother of August's, was living now—the farm about three miles straight north of Turkey Creek, the one with the small white house and the patch of timber. It had all been timber in those days.

The Kaetterhenrys had not been among those whom Henry Baumgartner had brought to this region—they came a few years later—but their history was not very different from that of many families in the community. They came to this country from Germany in about 1849 or 1850, Casper and his wife and two children, and his brother Adolph and his wife. Casper's wife's brother, Johann Rausch, had preceded them. He was one of those who had drifted over into Iowa from Ohio or New York, coming because others were coming, because everyone was talking about the West. He had written back to his

17

relatives in the old country, full of enthusiasm, praising the country and telling how fine the land was, until he had got Casper and Adolph persuaded to come. ⋁

They landed at New Orleans after a voyage of eight weeks and three days in a sailing-vessel, and from there took boat up the Mississippi to St. Louis. They spent the winter there, waiting for spring. The older child, Joseph, died of cholera while they were there. Early the next March, as soon as the river was open, they again took boat, and went up as far as north-eastern Iowa. They bought oxen and farm implements at Guttenberg, the little river town where they landed, and from there went straight over to Turkey Creek to join Johann. He soon after pulled out again and went on West, but Casper and Adolph took up land near each other. Casper started right in clearing his land and putting up the log cabin in which the family lived until the children were good-sized.

The cabin had one room at first; later, two more were added. They did their cooking, eating, sleeping all in there. There the children were born, one after another—Mina, Kurt, Mary, August, Sophie, Heinie, Ferdinand.

18

They had had only Lena when they came there, since little Joseph had died on the way. They lived all crowded into that little cabin, four children sleeping packed into a dusty feather-bed over which the covers were hastily drawn in the day-time. Feather-beds and pillows and a little black tea-pot with raised blue flowers were all that the Kaetterhenrys had brought with them from the old country. They had had none of the "comforts of life" to begin with. They had saved up just money enough to pay for the journey and their first crude farming-necessities. They went through all the hardships of pioneer life, the clearing of the land, storms that killed their cattle and flooded their fields, the terrible blizzards of those days. Another child—Mary —died, and was buried in a little grave that Casper himself dug in a corner of their land. They had to work, all of them, father, mother, girls, and boys, just as soon as they could get into the field.

But they were a sturdy tribe: they could stand things. Casper Kaetterhenry had been a farm-labourer in the old country. He had always worked hard, and so had his wife. But now that he was working for himself instead of

19

for some wealthy Pomeranian landowner who would get all the profits, he was willing to work. Now he was going to make a landowner of himself.

He brought up his children to know very little but work. The mother had little time for them. In the intervals of bearing them she had to work in the field. So did Lena, the oldest girl. Mina gave them all the care that was given. They always cared more for this sister, in a way, than for any other human being—Mina, a thick-faced, heavy, "Dutchy"-looking girl, slow and melancholy and conscientious and kind. She afterwards married Rudy Nisson, and had a hard time of it.

The older children had no chance for any schooling, but a school-house was built on the outskirts of Turkey Creek to which the younger ones went off and on, as they could be spared, in the winter. That Turkey Creek school! It had wooden benches and a great stove on which one of the teachers—"Old Man Bartlett" they called him—kept hickory switches drying. Teachers were as irregular as pupils. Old Man Bartlett stayed only one week. He had already "licked" all the boys once or twice over, and he celebrated

20

his last day by whipping every one of the girls.
The next Monday he did not appear. He had
"skipped the country." He had come to Turkey
Creek from no one knew where, with only the
clothes on his back, and no one ever learned what
had become of him. There were a few attempts
made to hold a German school, but they did not
come to much. But it seemed to Casper Kaetterhenry that his children were in clover. He himself could do little more than write his own name.
Even some of the other farmers about there said
that Casper wasn't easy on his children. He expected them to work and that he should get all
the benefit of their work. As soon as they were
old enough to do anything, they had to help on
the farm. That was the way to save up money.
Casper kept them at it every minute.

As soon as August was eleven he began "hiring
out" to some of the neighbouring farmers. He
was a good worker. All of the Kaetterhenrys
were. "*Ach*, those Kaetterhenrys!" people
would sometimes say, meaning that they were
stubborn and silent and *dumm*. And of Kurt or
August or Heinie, "*Ja*, he's a Kaetterhenry all
right." They were Pomeranians. "Pummers"
people called them, making fun of some of their

21

ways and the queer Low Dutch expressions that old Casper used. But August was good help. He could do nearly everything about a farm that a man could.

He worked for all kinds of people. For Schumacher once, and for Grobaty, a fat, black-bearded old German who beat his wife and his horses and was converted regularly at every camp-meeting. Grobaty's father lived with him. He had an immense white beard that reached below his waist. Usually he kept it buttoned inside his coat, but sometimes August would see him lift it out and fondly stroke and caress it. August tried blacksmithing for a while, too, but he liked farming better. He would go back to school in the winter-time, but when he was fourteen he quit for good.

By the time that he was fifteen he was virtually on his own resources. He did not get on well with his father. August had a temper and he didn't stand the old man's tyranny. August was the pick of the family, most people thought. He was not so slow as the rest of them, although he had all of the Kaetterhenry stubbornness. There was more of the mother in him. There was a different strain in the Rausches. They

22

were more restless, more ambitious. People said
that Mrs. Kaetterhenry might have liked to have
things a little different from what they were at
home if it hadn't been for "him." She was not
a "Pummer." August was more like her. He
looked like her, too, with a fresh-coloured skin
and blue eyes showing temper in the way that
they were set. Sophie, too, was "a Rausch."

It was mostly work in those days, but there
were other things. Weddings were made much
of in that community. Sometimes the celebration lasted three days, like Hans Nisson's wedding, at the end of which most of the men were
laid out on the straw in the barn, dead drunk.
There was still more intoxication at the camp-
meetings which were held in the timber by travelling evangelists. People drove to them from
miles around, camping out in the woods and
attending the meetings. They were times of
religious debauch. The shouting and singing
and weeping, the general wallow of emotionalism, gave an outlet after all the hard, grinding
work. August "went forward" at one of these
meetings, along with the other young men, stirred
and yet shamefaced at the same time. He
believed that he was "converted."

23

Country People

Most of the life of the community centred about the German Methodist church out in the country, which Henry Baumgartner helped them to build. It was a plain white frame-building, bleak and small, a long hitching-board in front of it, and behind it the sheds for the teams and the two tiny outhouses all standing stark on a great clearing. Church was held in the afternoon. The farmers drove there in lumberwagons, tying their horses to the long hitching-board, or in bad weather putting them in the sheds. They stood about on the church-steps, talking, the men together and the women in another group, until the preacher drove up. Then they all marched solemnly into the church. The congregation sat, the men and boys on one side, the women and girls on the other, facing the pulpit—a silent, stolid congregation, moving slowly and heavily in dark garments, creaking awkwardly as they turned to kneel on the hard wooden floor, some of the men poised precariously on their haunches, muttering the Lord's Prayer together in a guttural German that was loud in the silent country church, the women's voices a husky murmur above the deep, shamed rumble of the men's.

They had no regular pastor. Sometimes Wilhelm Stille, a farmer from over near Richland who "did some preaching," came. He was a thin, fervent man, with a greyish beard and long hair, who leaned over the pulpit and spoke in a high, thin voice, his deep-set brown eyes burning with a kind of mystic ardour. Sometimes they had one of the travelling preachers, old exhorters, who wept and paced the platform as they prayed for sinners, and pounded the Bible.

After the service the people went outside and talked a little before they drove home. It was for this that the young men came. They stood about in abashed Sunday-constrained groups, pretending to talk to one another, but aware of the girls, whose eyes were aware of them; in their thick, dark best clothes that made their skin look leather-brown, their brown and black felt hats, their feet clumping awkwardly in stiff Sunday shoes. This group of boys and young men was the last to disperse. The older people talked in German, about the weather and the crops. Then the men went out to get the teams hitched up to drive home.

August stayed around Turkey Creek until his

mother died. She had been ailing for years, had bought "herb" medicine and liver pills and tonics from the medicine-man who drove around to the different farms with a horse and wagon selling remedies. No one had known what it was except stomach trouble, or had thought much about it. She had kept on working all the time. But finally, when she was almost confined to her bed, could digest virtually nothing, and could hardly drag herself into the kitchen to see how Mina, whom they had called in, was doing the work, Casper thought it might be time to drive into town and have the doctor come out with him. Of course it was too late then. Otherwise it would have been foolish for the doctor to be called. He too muttered something about stomach trouble, but the neighbour women who came in whispered "cancer" to each other. The children were sent for, and stood in awkward panic about the old walnut bed where their mother lay "wasted to a shadow," as the neighbour women said. The children had not actually realized that there was anything the matter with her until now. She died, and was buried in the little Turkey Creek cemetery near the German church.

The Kaetterhenrys

"Ach, that old Kaetterhenry!" the women said. "He worked her to death, and then what did she have!" She had not lived to enjoy anything from all her toil. They had been for a few years in the new frame-house, but she had had to do things as she had always done them before.

It was expected that Mina would stay on at home and keep house for the old man, at least until Heinie, who worked on the home place, brought home a wife; Rudy Nisson was drinking and could not be counted upon to support Mina. But this was not at all what old Casper had in mind. A few weeks after his wife had died, he offered ten dollars to anyone who could find him a new wife; and astonishingly, gross and hard-fisted and stingy as he was, a fat old man with a rough beard who went around in his bare feet, a tolerably fair-looking young woman was found for him. He had never spent anything and he owned a good farm now. Poor Mina knew nothing of all this until he brought the new wife home; then she had to leave. Rudy was off in the next town, supposed to be working, and she had nowhere to go and no money to keep her. She had to stay at Sophie's until Sophie's

27

husband could get Rudy to come back and find some sort of home for her. The new mistress proved to be very different from the old one: she made the old man Kaetterhenry stand around —build an addition to the house, get her some decent furniture. You never caught her working in the fields!

The children were furious. They talked about the insult to their mother and the injustice to Mina, but greed was at the bottom of it. This woman was a schemer; they could see that. Sophie declared that she looked like the kind of woman who would go about having children right away and beat the rest of them out of what was theirs by rights. What she had wanted was to get the farm left to her. It made them all angry to see how much she got from the old man while they, who had had to work like dogs for him from the time they were babies, got nothing. What had he ever done for them? It broke up the family and started a feud that still lasted after the old man Kaetterhenry had died and one of his sons by the second wife had the farm. But she did not get everything. Schemer that she was, she could never get old Casper to make

28

a will, and the children came in for some of his property.

Most of the Kaetterhenry children married young and settled down to farming right where they were. August was the only one who did not. Sophie had married a Klaus, and her brother-in-law, young Herman Klaus, had gone up to Richland to work. August liked what he heard of the Richland neighbourhood. He wanted to get into a better community; he thought he could earn more up there. He went there and got a job with a wood-choppers' gang in the winter, and the next spring he hired out to Henry Baumgartner.

This old Henry Baumgartner was harder to work for than any man in that part of the country. August found that out soon enough. It was not for nothing that he was as rich as he was. He was worth at this time about a hundred thousand dollars in land and money, considered rich for a farmer in those days, but no one would ever have guessed it from the way that the family lived. The old lady Baumgartner hoarded the bread until it was mouldy. It was said that she was still wearing the same clothes in which she had come over from Germany. It was not until they moved into town and the children got hold of some of the money that it began to show. Old Baumgartner was inconceivably mean in petty things. August remembered about Mrs. Hooper, a widow in Richland who supported her family by doing washing. She wanted a little straw to pack about her house in the winter-time, and Henry Baumgartner promised that he would bring her some when he next came into town. Then he charged her not only more than the price of the straw, but for his time and for the hauling, although he had been bringing in other things at the same time. Plenty of farmers, as he knew very well, would have been glad to give the poor woman that little bit of straw for nothing.

Yet he had his big, effusive side. August had seen him at the camp-meetings groaning and praying and exhorting, tears running down the side of his fat nose and soaking into his beard. He was about sixty at this time, short, bulky, with a thick, square-cut beard, a broad smooth German under lip that showed his emotionalism, and mean little eyes. Afterwards, when he moved into Richland and joined the Methodist

church there, he ran the church. The preachers
looked upon him with fear as he sat short, heavy,
belligerent in the front pew—he was getting
deaf—giving little grunts of disapproval or
breaking out into sonorous "Amens!" following
the emotional parts of the sermon with a running comment of groans, head-shakings, tears.
A terrible figure, with his big head and square-
cut, bushy beard showing that wet, shining lower
lip, the ominous glare of his small eyes. He was
sincere, more than sincere, in all this. It was
life to him. Plenty of people hated him, but
they spoke of him as the most religious man
around there.

If August managed to stick at the Baumgartners', he would be the first hired man who had
ever done so. But August was a sticker. People soon found that out. He had no intention
of leaving until he was ready to go. He went
stolidly about his work from four o'clock in the
morning until nine at night. He knew what he
was after. All the time he was saving part of
of his wages, putting some away. He did not
intend to let old Henry Baumgartner's meanness
drive him out until he had saved enough to start
in farming for himself. It was that for which
he was working.

III: *Emma Stille*

AUGUST liked the new community. He saw that in some respects it was ahead of Turkey Creek. For one thing, there was a railroad, a main line of the Illinois Central that connected Richland directly with Chicago. It would be easier to market crops here. There would not be so much hauling to do. It was only eleven miles from "Wapsie," the county seat, and that was an advantage. And, then, he liked the looks of the country. There was not so much timber, more prairie-land; and after all the clearing that he had had to do about Turkey Creek, August was not fond of timber. He said little, but he made up his mind before very long that he wanted to get hold of some land about here and settle down. Someone would be wanting to sell and move out. He had been saving ever since he started working for other people and was putting away some all the time. When he saw a good piece of land

32

he was going to try to get it, paying for it gradually as he could. And he had his eyes open for some girl who looked as if she would make him a good wife.

There were not so many Germans here as around Turkey Creek, and there were some Lutherans among them, so that they had no German Methodist church. Those who were close enough drove over to the Turkey Creek church when the weather was good. Most of them began "going in town." They drove to the Richland church, four of them together, two girls and two boys, in a two-seated buggy. The old people did not care to go there because the services were in English. They thought that it meant, too, that the young people were getting away from them.

There were more good times not connected with the church than there had been at Turkey Creek. Socials at the country schools, bob-rides, and big country parties where they played the old country games and kissing-games until the whole thing ended in a general "spooning," with the lights out. August was bashful. Herman Klaus urged him to get a girl and come on. But he did not go to these parties very much

33

until he began keeping company with Emma Stille.

That was in the first summer after he came to Richland. Henry Baumgartner let him go over to help the Stilles at threshing-time. The Stille boys had come over to help the Baumgartners. The Stille farm was about two miles from where August was working.

Old Wilhelm Stille was the one who used to preach in the Turkey Creek church. He was a gentle, dreamy kind of man. His threshing was always left until near the last. But old lady Stille saw to it that he did not get too far behind. People spoke of her as "someone to watch out for." She was short, squat, heavy. She had a round, wrinkled, crafty face with narrow, suspicious eyes. She looked as if she might just have come from the old country. She parted her hair smoothly in the middle and wore round ear-rings. When they drove into town, she never wore a hat, but a dark scarf tied over her head. Her dark, thick, shapeless clothes, her shawls, her scarf, her soft felt slippers, all added to the feeling of craft, of slyness, that she gave. People were afraid of her. She was stingy, too,

34

as stingy as the Baumgartners; but the girls saw
to it that the threshers were well fed.

There were two of the Stille girls at home,
Emma and Mollie. Herman Klaus liked Mollie
Stille pretty well. Everyone liked the Stille
girls. They said that they were just nice girls,
not so queer as their father and without their
mother's meanness. They waited on the table
when the threshers came. The men all knew
them and joked with them. August had nothing
to say, but he knew every move that Emma Stille
made as she hurried around the long table bringing in more stewed chicken and coffee. She was
not very large, but she looked like a good worker.
Her black hair curled a little from the heat, and
her face was flushed. Her lips, full German
lips, curved, dark red, were slightly parted.
The men teased her. "Hurry up there, Emma!
Emma, you're too slow!" August sat eating
industriously, without looking up; but when
Emma came near him and put out her hand to
take his coffee-cup, he caught the faint scent of
heat that came from her, saw the little beads of
perspiration about the roots of her shiny black
hair.

35

He liked her. He wondered if she was pretty strong. She seemed to be able to get through with a lot of work. She did not look in the least like her mother. She was a giggler; she and Mollie both could seem to giggle by the hour, but just the same she was pretty sensible. She taught country school in the Benning Township school-house, but she knew how to wait on threshers.

The old man Stille was not badly off despite his preaching. He had come out in an early day and had managed—he and the boys together—to get hold of a good deal of land. He had helped the boys, and he ought to be able to help the girls a little, too. The Stille girls would have had more beaus if the young men had not been afraid to get mixed up with that old lady. She was down on all her daughters-in-law. That would not stop August. He'd like to see any old woman that could bother him very much.

The threshers were at the Stilles' two days. It was in early September, dry, burning weather, when the bright new evergreens in the grove at the north of the house stood motionless and pointed against the blue sky. The men worked with their old horse-power thresher out in the

36

fields, where the stubble was bright and harsh
under their feet and the sun blazed on the
yellow-gold straw-stacks that piled up behind
the machine. Emma and Mollie came out once
to see them work. Some of the men stopped for
a moment and "joshed" with them, offered to let
them run the machine, told them they ought to
be out here helping thresh instead of sitting
around the house doing nothing.

"*Ja*, doing nothing!" the girls scoffed. "I
guess we'd see what would happen if you didn't
get any supper to-night."

"Oh, do *you* get supper?" Herman Klaus
said. "I thought your ma did that, and you
girls set around looking nice." They struck out
at him until he backed off from them, holding up
his hands and shouting, "Hey! Hey! I gotta
work! Owgust, come here once and help!"

August was too bashful yet to join in. He
pretended not to notice, but he saw the girls,
standing there leaning against each other, half
closing their eyes against the sun, which was
bright on their black hair and flushed cheeks, the
blue dresses against the blazing gold of the
straw-stacks and the stubble out under the blue
prairie-sky. The chaff filled the air, and the

ask the two Stille girls to go to the Fourth of July celebration at Richland Grove.

They started early and called at the Stille place for the girls. They had hired a team. They wore their best dark, thick suits, which made their hands and necks look browner. The girls wore striped summer dresses with tight basques, and Mollie had fastened a row of "spit-curls" across her forehead. August did the driving. Emma sat on the front seat beside him, and Herman and Mollie were "cutting up" in the back seat, Herman shouting, "Now, Emma, you make that Owgust act decent up there in front, where I can't look after him."

"You better act decent yourself," Emma retorted. August blushed furiously.

The big wooden gate of the grove was propped open. "This way, boys!" a man shouted jovially. They drove in slowly over the fresh wheel-marks that had smoothed down the long green grass and looked around for a place to tie. The buggy-wheels scraped over a stump half hidden in the grass, lifting up the buggy on one side and making the girls squeal. They stopped. No one seemed to know just what to do.

"Well, might as well get out," Herman said.

"What you girls sitting in here for?" The girls stood aside while the boys staked out the horses. Then they all wandered off together, not knowing just what to do now that they were here. There were bunches of girls going around together, children darting off and being hauled back, women shrieking, "Come here, Mister! You don't get away yet. Come back here and fix this swing."

The grove had been well cleared of underbrush, and there were open spaces through which the sun shone golden-green. There were burr-oaks in clumps, larger oaks standing apart, full-leaved, casting a gracious shade. The ground lay in smooth, rounded slopes with long fine green grass that was full of little whirring things. It was sprinkled with wild gooseberry bushes, bitter-smelling white yarrow, clumps of catnip filled with black-bodied wild bees. The creek was dry, a narrow stream bed filled with hot white sand. Some children were running along it with bare feet.

There were swings put up, games going on. Rigs were standing all about: wagons, buggies of all descriptions, a carryall. Horses, big farm horses, were staked out with ropes. They would

41

begin to eat the bark off the trees, and then the
men would have to run up and tie them somewhere else. There were family groups, old
ladies sitting on cushions or in buggies, un-
attached boys going about hoping to find girls,
men pitching horseshoes. The four young
people were glad when it was time for the
program.

The speaker's stand was built of fresh new
planks, with a resiny scent, bound around
with red-white-and-blue bunting. There was an
amphitheatre of planks laid across low saw-horses.
August and Herman and the two girls stood at
the edge of the crowd. There was a smell of
perspiring people, cloth, starched dresses, planks.
Babies cried. The chorus sang patriotic songs.
A strong, fierce-looking girl went pounding to the
front of the platform and declaimed "Barbara
Frietchie" in a loud, coarse voice. When she
came to "Dame Barbara *snatched* the silken
scarf," she caught up the flag and waved it
wildly. Some people clapped, others looked
half gratified and half foolish. The chorus sang
again, "We're tenting to-night on the old camp
ground." Despite harsh untrained voices, there
was something touching about the sad cadences,

42

sung there in the open, breezy grove. State
Representative Calkins, from "Wapsie," spoke.
There was a scraping and moving-about when he
first came forward, and then a long silence before
he began. He spoke loudly, but it was hard to
hear him. The breeze seemed to carry his voice
away from all except the people directly in front
of him. The children were still playing in the
swings. Young people who did not care about
speeches, the oak leaves rustling, the horses, the
whispering on the outskirts of the audience,
drowned the speech. Herman and Mollie got
tired of it and slipped away. August and
Emma felt foolish when they saw that the others
had gone. Emma's brother, Willie Stille, was
in the chorus, and he sat up there grinning at
them.

They sat near the buggy to eat their lunch.
Emma and Mollie had brought a huge lunch in
a big red pasteboard box. The table-cloth was
hunched up in places by little spears and bunches
of grass. But eating seemed to dispel their
awkwardness.

After dinner the boys went away for a while
and pitched horseshoes. The girls went to sleep,
and awoke with hot, shiny faces. They took

43

down their hair, and were just putting it up again when the boys came back. They squealed. The boys teased Mollie about her spit-curls until she got angry and threw them away. Herman put them on and pranced around, and then he had to go after Mollie and make peace. August and Emma sat down on the buggy-robe on the grass. August took off his heavy felt hat. There was a white band of flesh that shaded into red-brown below the golden roots of his hair. The oak leaves rustled dreamily.

August and Emma wandered off together. They crossed the hot white stream bed and climbed the hill, sat down in the shade between some trees and gooseberry bushes. Emma picked some of the gooseberries to take home, and August helped her pull off the woody little hulls. He put his hand over hers in the grass. The hand quivered, and he held it closer, his hard brown fingers grasping a little higher on the wrist. There was an exciting incongruity between their halting self-conscious talk and the warm, thrilling animal intimacy of their hot, moist palms in the long fine grass. The shouting from the races down on the level ground came to them long-drawn-out and dreamily

44

distant. They were aware of the little green things that jumped about in the grass and of the heat of their two hands on the cool earth near the grass roots.

When they went back, Mollie and Herman were sitting in the buggy "spooning."

August made Herman drive home He and Emma sat in the back seat. Herman kept saying, "Why are you two so quiet back there?"

"*Ach*, you shut up, and tend to your driving." August put his arm around Emma. She took off her hat and put her head against his shoulder. The weeds along the roadside were damp, and wet night odours and mists came up from the fields. There was nothing but riding, jolting on through the dusk, the horses' hoofs pounding on the hard road, the buggy-wheels scraping.

After that August and Emma "kept company right along." The old lady Stille made little trouble, for she wanted her girls to be married. Wilhelm Stille promised to let them go on one of his farms, the one between Richland and "Wapsie," with the privilege of paying for it gradually. Emma did not teach country school the next year, but stayed at home getting ready to be married. The wedding would be as soon

45

as August had enough saved to start them out on the farm.

The first day that August could get away they drove into "Wapsie." The four of them again, in the Stilles' two-seated buggy, August and Emma and Herman and Mollie. It was late February, just before the last thaw. The road to "Wapsie" was a winter study in dull black and white. The snow, which had an opaque, thick look under the colourless winter sky, drifted down the black earth of the slopes; the plum-trees in interlaced masses along the creek, low, spreading, done in smoky black, purple tinging the massed farther trees and the bushes; the creek half under thin greyish ice cracked and broken down in places; the road dead black, sifted over with fine snow. The buggy looked small on that great expanse of land, the hoofs of the horses on the hard wintry road made a lonesome sound.

The town had a closed-up winter look. The girls did not speak as they drove along the wintry street. They sat small and subdued in their heavy country wraps and dark knitted hoods. They drove to the court-house. The two boys tramped solemnly into the old brick building,

46

with its dusty wooden floors and brown spittoons
and glimpses of littered rooms, with shelves stuck
full of records. August got the licence of the
county clerk, a little crippled man with one
shoulder higher than the other.

Then they drove to the minister's house.

The girls got out of the buggy and stood stiffly
on the board side-walk while the boys tied the
team to a wooden hitching-post. All four went
solemnly up the walk to the house. They did
not know whether to knock or to open the storm-
door. No one heard them at first, and they went
into the chilly, bare little entry, where overshoes
and a fibre mat were piled, until August finally
rang the bell.

"Ring again once," Emma whispered.

The minister's wife came, tall, gaunt, with
spectacles. She said in a businesslike way:

"Did you wish to see Mr. Taylor? Step
inside."

They filed silently into the parlour. They
sat waiting, the girls clasping their hands
nervously, staring at the hard-coal burner, the
lounge, the pink sea-shell on the stand.

The minister came in with hastily brushed
hair. They sat in frozen embarrassment.

47

"Is there anything I can do for you?"

August cleared his throat resolutely. He and Herman had been turning their caps on their knees, with hands red from the cold.

"We came to get married. If you——"

"Oh, certainly, certainly," Mr. Taylor assured them hastily.

Mrs. Taylor had thought "wedding" when they first came in, and had come back into the room. Now she asked the girls if they would not like to take off their wraps. She offered to let them go into the bedroom "if they wanted to fix up any," but they shyly refused. August asked her where the kitchen was, and after he had washed his hands at the granite basin, he came back and murmured, "Do you want to wash up, Emma?"

After many backings and exchanging of places, with a nervous determination on Mr. Taylor's part to mistake Mollie for the bride, which made Herman blush, the wedding party was arranged. August and Emma stood between the two windows, with Herman and Mollie in frozen attitudes on each side of them, and Mr. Taylor facing them.

"Dearly beloved, we are gathered together in the presence of God and these witnesses to join this man and this woman in the holy bonds of matrimony."

The voice sounded sonorous in the small, bleak room. Emma stood in trembling quietness. August had to clear his throat, and then his voice came out gruffly. Herman breathed hard and eased his weight. Some coal dropped in the stove.

They felt shy and happy under the congratulations of Mr. and Mrs. Taylor. They signed the certificate, and August fished in his pocket and brought out two dollars for the minister. Emma said that they would bring his wife a chicken in the summer.

They drove back to the farm down the dim, chilly road, the bare bushes thin and small, the fields spreading out black and sprinkled with snow. There was a wintry red in the Western sky.

They had supper at the Stilles', where the old lady had got up a big meal for them, inviting in all the married children. Emma was to stay there until August "got things fixed" at the farm

49

and could come after her. But he had to go straight over to the farm in the morning. One of the Stille boys was staying there now, looking after things, but the next day August was to take possession.

Part Two

I: The Farm and the Children

THE farm, when August and Emma first went there, didn't look much as it did later. It was one that Wilhelm Stille had got hold of almost by accident through a mortgage. It had had a poor owner, and then renters on it, so that it was in bad shape. Willie Stille had been "batching it" there during the winter months, but of course he knew that he wasn't going to stay, and had done no more than keep things going. But it was a piece of land that would pay the man who really took hold of it.

Few of the present improvements were there. The buildings were flimsily built affairs, some of them unpainted. There was a little one-story house with old-fashioned small-paned windows, dismal and dark and ugly. No yard, no bushes or flowers, and over on the west a tangled, half-grown wilderness of all kinds of trees and bushes planted together. August cut all those down

53

later, except the double row of elms that he left
for a wind-break. One thing there was, a good
well. Otherwise it was like building a place up
from the beginning.

The old lady Stille would have liked to keep
the farm in her own hands, to have had August
and Emma stay there merely as renters. She
liked to keep a hold on the children. But
August would not go there under any such
conditions. He meant to work without stopping
until he had paid for the farm. He had a
genuine Kaetterhenry obstinacy and a desire to
do things for himself. He would not stand
interference; his mother-in-law soon found that
out.

The Kaetterhenrys started in with almost
nothing, as most young couples did in those days.
August had something saved from all his years
of work; Emma did not know exactly how
much. He spent this very thriftily. At first
they would have to get along with as little as
they could, "until they got the farm paid for."
He paid for part of his stock and implements and
went in debt for the rest. To have a farm free
from encumbrances; to own "clear" the stock,
the machinery, and the land, was what he was

54

working for. All that he had or could make
went into the farm.

The house—*ach*, that didn't matter so much.
It was a gloomy, bare little house. Emma
brought along what she could from home: com-
forters that she and her sisters had been making
through the winter; some goose-feather pillows;
rag rugs that she had sewed; some heavy white
dishes, with a brown rim, and a clover leaf in
the centre, that she and Mollie had picked out
in the store in Richland. August and Emma
drove into town one day and got what furniture
they would need: a black walnut bed and commode; a kitchen table and stove; chairs; a
parlour stand. There were wedding presents.
Emma's father gave them a clock, and her
mother a feather-bed. Hans Stille, who was
known as "quite a carpenter," made them a tall
narrow desk and bookcase of home-grown black
walnut. August's sister Mina sent them a
"splasher" for the commode on which she had
worked in red outline stitch some ducks and
waves. The Stille boys gave them an album
with orange plush covers, and Mollie and Herman Klaus, who were going to be married soon,
bought them a set of vases, with cattails encrusted

in gold on the sides. Their living was done in the kitchen and bedroom. The front room, which had the rag carpet, the stand, the vases, and the album, and a large German Bible, they kept shut off.

They could not afford help. August did most of the work himself. He got up at daylight, or earlier, and it was dark before he finished his chores in the evening. He was "one of the best workers around," people said. He was going to have a good place here some day. One or another of the Stille boys came over and helped when the work was heaviest. Emma had to help him in the field. August saw nothing unusual in that, although most of the farmers' wives here were not seen in the fields. All "the womenfolks" had had to help over in the Turkey timber. He had always seen his mother and his sister Lena out working with the men. He expected it of his "woman."

There was not much but work for them these days. They had no buggy at first, only a wagon. But they drove into church when they could on Sunday mornings. Church—that was somehow part of doing well, of living the way they should and getting prosperous. They couldn't go off

the place often, since they had no one to leave
with the stock. And when they did go, they
must always be back in time for chores. August
got away more than Emma did; he had trips to
make into town. Emma soon found out that he
was not the kind who would take her with him.
His mother had never gone to town. He did all
of the buying. He had a shrewd, hard feeling
that he must keep things in his own hands if he
was going to get ahead. He had that thrifty,
bull-headed Kaetterhenry streak in him that
showed in his attitude toward the woman.
Emma hated to ask him for things. She went
out to the wagon timidly, said, "August, do you
think you could get me a little of that calico,
maybe?" He grunted. He would get it if he
thought she needed it, but he decided that.

Emma settled down quickly into a young farm
wife. She "lost her giggles," as the family said,
and got an air of timidity that was an accentua-
tion of her old shyness. She was thin, with skin
burned dark, and tired, hollow eyes. She seldom got out of her wrappers. August was close;
he did not tell her things. He expected a good
deal of her. But, still, as her sisters told her
and as she knew, she had got a good man. He

would have a fine farm some day, and then she would be glad that they had worked while they were young.

Then the children were born, Frankie, Mary, Elva, Carl. That kept Emma busy enough. While she had only the first two, she still helped in the field. Frankie and Mary were easy to manage. But when Elva was born, Emma had a hard time. It had to be right in haying-time, the men there, and no one to feed them, no one to look after the other children. They got August's sister Mina, a fat, kind, melancholy woman now, who worked at anything that she could find to do; but the old lady Stille couldn't stand it to have any of August's folks there. She came over, "nosing in," as August said, and she drove out even Mina, who was used to all kinds of treatment. Emma had to get up before she was ready and go to work again. There was no time for rest these days, she said, even if a person was sick. But she was never quite so well from that time.

After the first two, she had to stop helping August outside. She still helped with the milk-ing, took care of the chickens and geese and the milk and cream, and made butter. She had all

that *she* could do in the house. Wherever she
went, the children were following her—in dingy,
much-washed blue dresses, made too large, so that
they could be handed along and fit the next one
—little, frowzy-headed country children, tod-
dling after her, pulling at her skirt, under her
feet wherever she stepped. The older ones could
play outdoors by themselves, but there was
always a baby in the red high-chair beside the
stove while she cooked or ironed; and she would
have to stop to change diapers, cry, "No, no, you
can't have that!" snatch the child hurriedly up,
murmuring, remorsefully but a little fretfully,
"Come on now. No, mamma ain't forgot all
about you. Did you think she had? Can't you
let mamma get back to her work now?" Sometimes she was fretful and anxious. But Emma
never seemed to get really cross. She never
sprang up and "took a whack at them," like
Mollie, and then got ashamed of herself.

Emma did not look so strong, but she could
keep going.

The two oldest children, Frankie and Mary,
had always been "real good." Emma had never
had any trouble with them when they were
babies. They were both quiet, slim, dark-haired

59

children, like some of the Stilles. They would always play together and amuse themselves, Mary especially. Mary was always a great one for school. When she was a tiny thing she used to play school out near the corn-crib, with the ears of corn, with their long silken hair, for "scholars," all arranged in a row before her, their hair braided, wearing little hats of leaves trimmed with clover blossoms, which she carefully removed when school began. She tried to read before she knew one letter from another; anything, the texts on the coloured Sunday-school cards, seed catalogues that came to the house, the labels on baking-powder cans. "She must be going to be a school-teacher when she grows up," people said.

Elva was the odd one. She didn't seem to belong to the rest of the family. Perhaps it was because she had been sickly when she was a baby and had had some "spoiling." She had been twice as much trouble as the other two put together. When she was a baby she used to have spells of holding her breath, and even her father had a hard time to manage her. She had fine, red-gold hair and a very white skin, although she

was never exactly pretty. She liked to get out
of things and to leave Mary to do them.

She still took more care than Carl, when he
was born three years later. Carl was the one
who took after his father most. He had the
light hair, ruddy skin, blue eyes, and was stocky
and sturdy. He kept things to himself, too.
Carl was August's favourite. August was never
much of a hand to be around the children, but he
paid more attention to Carl.

August wanted his children to have what other
children had, but he thought they ought to help.
Frankie had to help his father out in the field as
soon as he was big enough to go out there.
August wasn't going to pay for help when he had
boys of his own. "My, how those Kaetterhenrys
all work!" people would exclaim. They would
see this little fellow out in the field, in the burning sun, working just like a man. Looking like
a man, too, in his blue overalls and big straw hat,
It didn't seem to August that his children had it
hard. He remembered his own childhood and
how his father had made all of them slave. He
didn't work Frankie like that. August wouldn't
have thought of having Frankie go and hire out

off the place, as he had had to do. Frankie
didn't know what it was to have to get along as
his father had done at some of those places where
he had worked, Grobaty's, for instance, where he
used to sleep in the straw. August could not
see that he was hard on the boy. But other
people said that Frankie was a man before his
time. A short, dark, sober boy with brown skin,
always looking a little stunted, especially in that
best suit of dark, thick cloth, the blue tie, and
the brown felt hat, that he wore to Sunday
school.

August never required Mary to help on the
place, as his oldest sister had done. That hadn't
hurt Lena any. Look at her now, a big stout
woman, mother of seven children, stronger than
it seemed Mary would ever be. Mary was
obedient and good, and she was a great help with
the housework and the little ones. The trouble
with her was that she didn't have her mind on
what she was doing. She always had to have
her nose in a book, anything that she could get
hold of, the big German Bible, a "History of the
Civil War" that August was once inveigled into
buying from an agent, the mail-house catalogues.
Those catalogues opened up worlds to Mary.

The Farm and the Children

She could hardly wait for her father to go into town to the post office when it was time for a new one to come. She couldn't bear to go past anything that had printing on it. When they were driving along the road and saw a piece of newspaper, she would beg to get out and capture it. August thought this was silly. He could see no sense in a girl's wanting to read and study so much.

"*Ach*, what do you always have to be reading for?" the others said.

But the oldest girl in a family like theirs didn't get much chance to read.

The country school was two miles from the Kaetterhenry farm. August always "aimed" to let the children go. They walked the two miles back and forth, taking their lunch in tin pails. They went "pretty regular," except when they were needed at home, Frankie for the farm work and Mary to help with the babies. Elva didn't care much for school, but Mary made a terrible fuss, they said, when she had to miss.

That school seemed pretty fine to August when he thought of what he had had. That old Turkey Creek school with teachers coming and going! This was a nice frame building, painted

63

pink, with desks and seats like those in the town school. And then they had a teacher for the whole term. A high-school girl from Richland usually (the high school there gave a two-year course) who was teaching a few terms of country school before getting married. Mary was always talking about town school, but August couldn't see but that they got about as good as what they'd get in town. All they needed, anyway.

August and Emma wanted to do the best for their children that they could. It worried Emma that they couldn't always get in to Sunday school; that was more important than the other school. That was bringing the children up right. August bought a buggy so that he could take them. They drove in on Sunday mornings —August and Frankie on the front seat, in the back the two girls, and Emma holding little Carl on her lap. Often they got there too late for church, but they were in time for Sunday school. Mary and Elva in funny little dresses too long for them, stiff best hats with elastic under their chins, hair in tight black and blond braids tied with little pieces of narrow blue ribbon. Frankie clumping in heavy shoes that smelled of

blacking, looking too old for his age in his heavy
dark suit with "long pants" and a brown felt hat
like his father's.

They prized the coloured cards that they got,
with pictures and the golden text on them, showing Christ, with brown curly hair, in white robes,
the disciples in blue and red (blue for John, who
was pictured as almost as pretty as Jesus).
Their Sunday-school papers were treasured
during the week—*The Boy's Friend*, *The Girl's
Friend*, *Dew Drops*. Mary read the stories
avidly. Even Emma got into the habit of looking at the serials in *The Girl's Friend*, although
she never actually finished one.

The children were shy, and wouldn't say much
in Sunday school, Mary and Elva because of the
town girls, who wore better dresses than they did.
But they all looked forward to Sunday school,
loved the cards, the papers, the drive to town,
the hymns, jingly Methodist "Sabbath-school"
hymns, "There Is Power in the Blood," "Jesus
Paid It All," "The Old-time Religion." Mary
wished that they had an organ so that she could
learn to play these songs at home, and Emma
admitted wistfully that it "would be nice."
When they went to Henry Stille's, where there

was an organ in the closed, chilly front room, Mary went in and learned to "pick out the tune," or something like the tune.

"Until they got all this paid for once"—that was the answer to everything, new house, new furniture, organ.

The old Stilles did not like it very well that their grandchildren were going to "English church." August and Emma did not speak German in the home, as the old people had done.

"*Ach, das ist nicht recht!*" the old man Stille would say sadly. He wondered what would become of them all.

II: *Grandma and Grandpa*

THE house simply wouldn't hold them all. Three years after Carl there was Johnnie. And then the old Stilles wanted to give up their home and come to live with August and Emma. August hated to do anything with the house until he had a better barn, but there was no way out of it. The old Stilles would help a little.

Hans Stille was working over near "Wapsie." He was the only one who never married, a little, shy, dark-haired man with shining, dark-brown eyes and timid, gentle ways. Mary was like him in some ways, the Kaetterhenrys said when they were provoked at Mary. He never seemed to settle down and get anywhere, but there was not much in the line of handy things that he couldn't do. He stayed with August and Emma all that summer and the next. They moved back the old house, used the two old front rooms for kitchen and bedroom, and built on three new

rooms in front and an upstairs with two rooms.
It looked like a nice modern house when they got
through with it, although the upstairs was never
fully finished—white, with pink trimmings, a
narrow porch, a triangle of wooden lace under
the peak in front. The next summer Hans made
over the two old back rooms into a corn-crib and
tool-house.

Then there had to be new things for the house,
of course. They ordered some new furniture
from the catalogue, a combination desk and
bookcase for the front room (they used the old
one that Hans had made for a cupboard), a new
stationary rocker upholstered in green-flowered
velvet. They got a new bedroom set for themselves, dresser, commode, and bed of golden oak,
the bed with a high head-board. They put the
old walnut things in the boys' room, the big end
room, left half finished, used as a store-room, too.

When the old Stilles came they brought some
of their things with them,—their long extension
table and some chairs for the dining-room;
grandpa's old German books, queer ancient
things with faded black and brownish bindings,
religious books; some old home-made walnut
beds and feather-beds; ancient quilts of dark

68

woollen pieces. The little old downstairs bed-room in the back now became "grandma's and grandpa's room," a small, dark, stuffy room with an uneven floor, one dingy, small-paned window. They set up an ancient walnut dresser with a little dark-framed mirror hung above it, an old rope bed piled high with billowy feather-mattresses, with dark-looking musty-smelling quilts over them; and on nails in one corner, grandma's and grandpa's clothes—an old brown waistcoat, the coat in which grandpa had done his preaching, some big gaping country shoes, and grandma's dark dresses and stealthy-looking grey shawls and old black petticoats. The two big wooden rockers stood there, and beside one of them an ancient brown spittoon.

One thing that the old people brought was an organ. One of the old carpeted pedals would not work. It was put into the sepulchral front room, and August declared that he could pay for no lessons. But somehow Mary managed to pick out a few hymn tunes on it. Maybe some day some of them could "take."

The old people had had misfortunes. After getting together a good-sized pile of money from his land, grandpa had made poor investments.

Some he had lost in Colorado gold-mines; and a German Methodist insurance company advertised in the flaming German monthly which he took, *Die Flammende Fackel*, had swindled him out of more. His son Willie took the home farm, but some of the rent would have to go to make up losses. Old Wilhelm Stille had long been on the verge of joining a communistic colony in Wisconsin of some wild Methodist sect, but the old lady had kept him from it; and now that he had so little money to put into the common fund, the colony seemed much less eager to get him. So he went instead to his daughter Emma's. The old lady shrewdly suspected that her son-in-law August was likely to have the best home for them in the long run.

They moved over soon after the new house was finished. August was close, but he would do what he must. He realized that he owed some of his start to his wife's people, but he determined that the old lady should know her place.

The old folks were now "Grandma" and "Grandpa" Stille to everyone. They had aged greatly in the last few years. It seemed as if grandpa had changed, now that he no longer had farm affairs to attend to, and that his "religious side" had come uppermost. He was thin, with a lean face, a large nose, scant, straight silvery-white hair that grew long, a white beard, and deep-set, mystical, dark eyes. His thin voice was gentler, had a far-away sound. He was feeble, and when he first came, they feared that he wouldn't last long. He couldn't do much but sit in the wooden rocker with the calico cushion, smoking a black pipe and reading his old German religious books and papers.

The old lady was squatter, craftier-looking than ever, with that round, wrinkled face, the smooth hair showing the broad, worn white parting, the round ear-rings, her eyes now two slits in narrowed, lashless rims. She went softly about in slippers, in a shapeless dark-grey calico dress and dingy, black apron, a scarf tied over her head. At first she tried to run things. She tried to tell the children what they should do and she protested against every cent that the family spent, wanted them to live in every way just as she and grandpa had lived.

Emma was going to submit to grandma's interfering at first. The old lady had always had all of the children—and grandpa, too—

71

under her thumb, ruling them through their fear
of her meanness. But August had no intention
of letting grandma get the upper hand. He had
stood things from grandma before, when she had
come snooping over to see how they were running
the farm and to exclaim at the waste. But
things were changed now. He had finished
paying for the farm a good while ago, although
he had not actually admitted it to Emma, thinking the less the womenfolks knew about that sort
of thing the better. This was his own house
now. No woman was going to come around and
tell him how to run it.

Grandma soon found that there was one person
whom she couldn't rule. All her schemes, her
craft, her sullenness, and her tantrums, which
had always got her what she wanted as a last
resort, were powerless against August's stubbornness. She was a little afraid of August from the
start. She tried to get in her work without
August's knowing it, when he was out of the
house; but when he came in and found out what
she was up to, then there were battles. The
children sat in terrified, wide-eyed awe, and
Emma wept a little, silently and tremblingly,
while grandpa pleaded, moaning sadly, "Ma—

Mutter—ach, no! no! no!" The children had never seen anyone like grandma at these times. The old woman could be a fury. But August was stronger than she. She found that she could not conquer him as she had the others. She was reduced to impotence, to angry mutterings, while she eyed August with a bitter, vengeful, helpless glare.

She had always had sullen times when no one could do anything with her. She had them now —times when she would not eat or move or speak, when, after grandpa and Emma had vainly tried to call her to meals, the children were sent to the door of her room. They found her sitting there in her old wooden rocker in the gloomy, low-ceiled room, among her old household things and her shawls and dresses, a tragic, baffled, ominous old figure, shapeless and huddled together in her dark, dingy old clothes, with her feet in their spreading, black felt slippers, rocking, and muttering, in guttural German, things that they could not understand.

This was the only revenge against August that she had. He let her be when she was like this. But she knew that even in this she dared not go too far. August was the only one who had ever

been able to manage her. Far down underneath
her anger and bitterness there was a kind of
admiration of him. He was hard and thrifty
and strong and a good farmer. She secretly
despised her other son-in-law, Herman Klaus,
beside him—Herman, a little, dried-up, under-
sized man who let Mollie have the say-so.
August was not a "blower." He was close-
mouthed, and the old woman admired that.
And she secretly approved of his looks. You
could tell from them that not many people were
going to get ahead of him. Sturdy, square-set,
heavy, but not fat, in his old blue shirt and overalls, with his ruddy face and blue eyes and the
harsh outcropping of golden beard upon his sunburned skin, and the golden hairs on his thick
brown arms. His hair was not so heavy now;
there was a bald spot on top, but the old lady
thought contemptuously that he looked younger
than Emma did. She secretly thought that he
was too good a man for Emma, whom she considered weak and *läppisch.*

Having the old folks there made more work
for Emma. Her father she didn't mind. He
made no more trouble than he could help. He
tried to come out of his dreams to do what he

could for her. He gathered the eggs, helped to
hitch up the horses, kept the little ones out of the
way sometimes when she was busy. Marguerite,
the youngest, who was born after grandma and
grandpa came, was his favourite. A pretty,
wilful little baby, knowing very well that she
was the youngest and had privileges, with a fuzz
of golden curls and bright blue eyes. She was
the only child born in the new house, and she
seemed to come into a different order of things.
Even her father was less severe with her than
with the others. Grandpa put aside his old
papers, trotted her on his knee, sang old German
hymns to her in a faint high-pitched voice that
seemed to come from a different world, took her
out obediently to see the "calfies," made Johnnie
give up his playthings to her. Emma had plenty
to do besides, and was glad to have grandpa look
after Marguerite.

Grandma had always worked hard at home,
but she wanted to say how things should be done.
Here she complained that she was useless; no one
paid any attention to her. She would have
helped with the cooking. But, "*Ach*, I don't
know," Emma told Mollie. "Ma has her old
ways of doing things, and the children they don't

seem to like what she makes." She clung more
than ever to her old ways now, spoke almost
nothing but German, would not leave the place
or ride in the new buggy, would use none of the
"new-fangled" things except the telephone.
That was grandma's one solace. She could sit
"listening in" for an hour at a time, a look of
stealthy gratification on her face, hearing everything: her daughter Mollie call a neighbour,
Herman call in from town to Mollie and say
what he was going to buy for Sunday, long con-
versations between two country women, deals
between men. But they could never get her to
speak into the telephone herself.

Grandpa had been the one who was ailing
when the old people came. But, although he
stayed somewhat feeble and tremulous, when his
troubles and farm worries were off his shoulders
at last, he seemed to get better and sink into a
kind of irresponsible sweet content, dreaming,
reading his old books, playing with Marguerite.
It was grandma who was ailing now. They
didn't know what was the matter with her.
She took more and more looking after. One
morning when she got out of bed she fell, and
couldn't get up. They had to have August come

76

in and lift her. Afterwards they thought that
it must have been "kind of a stroke." She
seemed to get all right again, and yet they
thought that it was hard for her to lift her feet,
and that she mumbled a little sometimes when
she tried to talk. Always in Emma's mind was
the fear of the time when her mother might be
helpless, like the old lady Schuldt, and have to
be taken care of.

It all came on Emma. Grandpa helped a
little, but there was more washing, more cooking
and more cleaning. It seemed as if she lived
more than ever in the kitchen. Neighbours consoled her. "Well, now you can go more. You
can leave the children with grandma and
grandpa and get away." Maybe they did go a
little more than before. They had a nice, big,
leather-topped, two-seated buggy now. There
were the boys to help August with the chores, so
that he didn't have it all to do.

They went into church often on Sundays,
leaving the two smallest ones with grandpa.
August and Emma joined the Bible class, which
was taught by the Hon. H. G. Bossingham, who
had served a term as State representative and got
the "Honourable" before his name. August

never talked in the class, but he enjoyed it more than anything since he used to attend the old German country church near Turkey Creek. Emma liked it, but she didn't always feel like coming. Either she or Mary had to stay at home and see about the dinner, and it had better be she, since, if she came, she felt uneasy about grandma.

They had their outings, like the other country people. They drove in to the Fourth of July celebration at "Wapsie" on a blistering hot day, leaving their team and buggy at the park and tramping the burning streets, where red-white-and-blue bunting was hung between the telephone poles. A silent country party, ill at ease, the girls in home-made lawn dresses of blue, with cheap lace, the boys sunburned and short, like little old men in their heavy clothes and felt hats. The hot cement burned through their stiff Sunday shoes. They listened to the band concert and the speech in the park. They brought their dinner in a big pasteboard box, and they and Herman's family ate together on the grass, fried chicken, thick bread and butter, pickles, coco-nut cake. The children teased for ice-cream, which the Baptist Ladies' Aid were serving, but August said there were too many of them and that they had enough without. The children liked to come, but there was all that work beforehand getting up the big lunch and getting all the children ready, then looking after them while they were there and getting them all together to go home again. Emma and Mollie said that they'd almost as soon stay at home.

They went to the county fair, held every September in the fair grounds at "Wapsie." They drove, and Herman and Mollie drove, and they took big boxes of lunch again and ate together. The men enjoyed the races, but the women liked to go into the big, flimsy wooden building, where the fancy work and cooking-exhibits were held, walking about and looking and murmuring to each other, "There's Mrs. Lempcke's quilt. It didn't get a prize. Look at that big pincushion with the blue tag on it. Do you think that's so pretty as all that?" Mollie brought some things once or twice, but Emma said, "*Ach*, I ain't got time for all such things."

The children always teased for more money than August would give them—wanted lemonade and wanted to go into all the shows. The older

79

children now began to go by themselves. Mary and Elva went with two "fellows" in a buggy, and Frank teased for grandpa's old one-seated buggy so that he could take his girl. The parents would meet the young people about the fair grounds, four or six going around together, Elva always giggling and "carrying on" until Emma was ashamed of her. They saw them at the lemonade and the ice-cream stands, and saw them carrying toy balloons. But they never met Frank and his girl. They didn't know where those two kept themselves.

August and Emma never went anywhere without the children except once to "open-air conference" down in the Turkey timber. While they were gone, Elva and the two little ones came down with scarlet fever. Emma said she'd never try that again. It was worse than staying at home.

Then grandma had the "stroke" that they had all been looking for. She was completely paralysed, and never got out of bed again. She didn't seem to realize much, but she never let anyone but Emma do things for her, except that she wanted August to turn and lift her. She was in bed for five years.

Emma lived between bedroom and kitchen, the kitchen a narrow, low-ceiled room, calcimined in green, the little window with geraniums in tin cans looking out across the back yard to the small orchard.

Emma always said that these were the hardest years of all.

III: *Loosening up*

THINGS were a little easier after grandma's death. At first Emma could scarcely realize that she could really leave the place, that when she worked she needn't always have the feeling that she ought to go in and look at grandma. In a way she missed the fact that grandma no longer needed her. But grandma had scarcely been a person to anyone for the last five years—only a responsibility, a gnawing sense of worry under everything. Nearly all the feeling connected with grandma had been fear, defence, rebellion, care, worry. Emma could not help feeling the relief that slowly seeped through everything.

Grandpa they didn't mind, he made so little trouble. He stayed about the same, as Emma told people, except that he seemed in a way to have withdrawn himself to a greater distance, that he seemed to be living in some region of his own. Only when some old friend or neighbour

came out occasionally, and they got to talking
of religion, he would come out of his dreams.
They could hear him praying aloud in his room
sometimes, the children coming in wide-eyed and
whispering, "Mamma listen to grandpa in
there!" *"Unser Vater . . . in dem Himmel,"*
the German words sounding rich, feeling, even
in his thin, high-pitched voice, with long pauses
between. He sat nearly always in his own room.
Marguerite was bigger now, she didn't need him.
He looked just about as when he had first come
to the farm—tall, thin, bent, with his narrow,
lined face and white beard, thin, silvery hair,
his deep-burning, dark eyes.

August was getting a few things now. He
was putting improvements on the place. He
had put up the big new barn, and Hans Stille,
who was keeping some bees now and doing a
little farming over on the other side of Richland,
had come for the summer again and made over
the old buildings. August had all the farm
buildings painted white, but the house would
have to wait awhile for its new coat. They had
a good milk-separator now, and Hans had fixed
up a milk-house for them. August kept everything in fine repair. He kept all his machinery

under cover, had no old ploughs and shredders standing about in the grove, like Herman Klaus and some other farmers. But he did not do much to the house. He had put in a sink in the kitchen, with a wooden cupboard underneath, and a soft-water pump. That was about all.

August and Emma had been too busy really to know that they were getting older. They had to look at the children to realize that. Emma looked older. Her hair was getting grey. She had always been slender, but she began to take on flesh now. People joked her about it, said, "You're getting fleshy, ain't you? You must be makin' the girls do the work for you." She said, without rancour, that she guessed she'd always been on her feet too much to get any flesh before. She'd run it all off. It made her look older instead of younger, dumpy and shapeless and middle-aged. She had to put on glasses, too. She should have done so long ago. She ordered a pair from a man who came around with a little card testing eyes, and who fitted people out with glasses cheap. But when farmers who had known August Kaetterhenry around Turkey Creek happened to meet him in town, they said, "Well, you ain't got so much older a'ready, Au-

gust." He looked a little heavier, his neck
creased and red, but in general about the same.

It was the children who were changing.
Frank was a man now, they had to realize, although he was a short little fellow and didn't
look any older than Carl when you saw them out
in the field together. He had once wanted to
be a mechanic, but he had given up that notion
and was going to get married and settle down to
farming. He had been going with the same girl,
for five or six years now—Lottie Schenck, a
heavy, coarse, hard-working girl. People were
all asking when the wedding was to be.

August would miss Frank when he left the
place, but Carl and Johnnie would help.
Johnnie might take hold better if Frank wasn't
there to do things. He was the restless one.
Neither of the other boys could be relied upon
quite so much as Frank. They hadn't been
brought up to work so hard. But August always
believed that Carl would make a better farmer
than Frank when he settled down to it. It was
hard to tell about Johnnie.

Frank was looking around for a place to farm.
August was doing most of the looking, however.
He had always wanted to get hold of the next

piece of land, where those LaRues had lived, and now, finally, the last of them was pulling out and going to Colorado. He took the farm for Frank. Frank was to pay him back eventually in the form of rent. August wanted to see the boy get a good start. He might be realizing a little, although he didn't admit it, that he had been harder on Frank than on the other boys. And he didn't mind having that other two hundred acres. It was a good investment, and made him the owner of four hundred acres of the best land, all there together. It gave him an excuse, too, to say to the family, who were getting to want too many things, "Needn't ask for that until I've got back some of what I paid for Frank's farm."

Mary was the one who was giving them trouble. More than Elva now, who had been inclined to be wild and to run around with fellows whom her parents couldn't approve. Mary had always been such a good child except for that weakness for reading. The only time they had had any trouble with her had been when she'd been determined to study to be a teacher and to go to the little Methodist academy at Wesley. August had said that she could teach

86

country school without going there. He had too many children to send them away to school. She'd settle down and marry like the rest of them, and there'd be his money wasted. She had seemed to give that up and not to say anything more about it. She had taken to dressmaking a little, had gone about to the neighbouring farms as people called for her. Of course she hadn't made much at it, because she was just Mary Kaetterhenry, someone whom they all knew; but it had given her something to do and got that crazy notion out of her head.

But now she began to have some queer spells. No one knew what to call them. The neighbour women were all interested, wondered if they could be fits, wanted to know all the symptoms. She would get pale and seem to stiffen out. The neighbours all advised different things, brought over remedies that had helped them. August and Emma bought her large bottles of "nerve tonic" at the drug-store, but that didn't seem to help. They were frightened, even to the extent of hitching up and taking her in to old Dr. Bowen's office in Richland. He gave them a prescription, but he didn't seem to know much more than they did what was the cause of the

87

thing. They "kind of lost confidence in Bowen," they said. A neighbour told them about this new "rubber doctor" in "Wapsie," and how he had cured her brother's wife. Mary wanted to try him. They took her into "Wapsie." He told them that some bone was out of place and was pressing on a nerve; and although they didn't see how that had caused the spells, they thought they'd try him. He wanted Mary to come in twice a week for treatment. $1.50 a treatment, a lot of money to pay for that little rubbing, but they were worried now. For a time it seemed that the treatments were helping her. Then all at once she got worse than ever. They heard of a place over across the river in Wisconsin where they gave mud baths that were supposed to cure anything. Despite the expense, they sent her there. When she came back she was better—she had never been away from home before—but she was told to take it easy, not do much of the work.

It had shaken them up a good deal to have Mary go back on them. It made them more careful with the other children. Elva was going with Roy Robbins, but it didn't seem as if Mary was going to get married. They let her go over to visit her Aunt Sophie Klaus at Turkey Creek. Then August let her go in to Rapids City and take a sewing-course. That was the most like going away to school of anything she had ever had. She improved after that, but she was not strong. She was like Grandpa Stille, tall, slender, black-haired, with bright, shy, dark, intelligent eyes.

Elva married when she was just a girl. She had stopped the country school long ago. Her parents wondered how she would like it when she had everything to do herself. They thought that she and Roy would make a queer set of farmers. They were both so flighty. But they started in immediately to raise a family, and that steadied them down.

Elva was the one who complained most that the younger ones "had it pretty easy." It was true; August was not so hard upon Carl and Johnnie as he had been upon Frank. Things were easier on the farm. Carl and Johnnie didn't have to stay out of school and help with the farm work, as Frank had done.

Frank felt himself at a disadvantage with the younger boys. They grew up into big, blond, good-looking boys. They didn't mingle much

89

with the older ones. They kept to themselves
and seemed to enjoy things together. Frank
was a little shy with them because they had gone
to school so much more than he had. Frank had
had to quit the country school at what would
have been about the seventh grade in town.

The roads were better now. It was easier to
get about. There were more horses on the farm,
and there was grandpa's old one-seated buggy.
August let the boys take that and Nell, one of
the old horses, and drive in to Richland to school.
More and more country children were doing that
now that the high school gave a full course.
The boys took Marguerite as far as the country
school. She was too little to go into town yet,
and by the time that she was ready, probably
they would have this new consolidated school
against which August was voting because of the
taxes.

August didn't know how it would be in the
winter. The first winter the boys tried to drive
back and forth the five miles. The next year
they stayed in town until spring, at the Henry
Stilles', where they kept the fires going and
looked after the chickens and the cow and
chopped the wood. They could go to the high-

school parties, and play basket-ball, go around
with the town "kids." Johnnie had a town girl,
and so did Carl part of the time. But he still
went to see Clara Josten, in the country, when he
and Johnnie went home on Friday night, and he
took her to box socials in the country schools.
August grumbled about the boys—*ach*, they
thought they had to have everything; didn't
know anything but basket-ball any more. But
he was proud of them.

It was entirely different with Marguerite than
with the older girls. She had everything, it
seemed, that Mary and Elva hadn't had. Elva
grudged it to her, said, "I'd like to see what pa
would have done to us if we'd asked for just half
the things she does!" But she was so much the
youngest, the baby and the pet, that it seemed
natural that they should give her things. Mary
made all her clothes for her, fitting her out
regularly every spring and fall, and watching the
dresses of the little girls at Sunday school to get
ideas for her. They liked to "dress baby up."
The whole family were proud of her hair, a thick,
blond fuzz that couldn't be braided, and at
which everyone looked, saying, "Hey, there,
curly-head!" They all knew that "baby" could

91

get things out of August. He grumbled, but when he knew that the cloth that Mary wanted to buy was to make "baby" a dress, she was sure to get it. He even let Marguerite take lessons on the organ from Miss Grace Brace-bridge, who drove about through the country with a pony and buggy teaching music.

August listened to the younger boys as he had never done to Frank, although he was still close and kept things in his own hands. The boys saw how other people did things. They tried to get their father to "loosen up a little," to get things that other farmers were getting. When they talked with their mother about it, she said, looking frightened, "*Ach*, how can we afford all that?" The boys hadn't grown up with any such awe of money matters. Emma had no idea of what the family resources were; she would never have dared to ask. But the boys seemed to know, somehow or other, what their father could do, how much he had. They scoffed, to Emma's scared delight, and said, "Aw, pa could have lots of things if he'd just loosen up and get them. We don't need to do things this way. Pa's so afraid he's going to take a cent out of the

bank. He's got more than most farmers have.
He could put up a silo if Uncle Willie did.
Why couldn't he?" *"Ach!"* Emma said,
frightened; but it pleased her.

They were beginning to get things. August
began to try out new machinery. He put up a
silo. One thing meant another. The boys kept
talking gasolene-engines. It was crazy to pump
all their water and turn the separator by hand.
They couldn't get August to say anything.
They needn't think that he would do whatever
they wanted. But he had been talking to Art
Miller in Richland, who was handling the Porter
lights, and one summer he had his own electric
plant installed on the farm. He didn't have
the house wired at once, but they had lights in the
barn and ran all their machinery by electricity.
August wanted his farm to have what other
farms had, but he hated to dig into that pile in
the bank. He knew how much work it had
taken to put it there. No one worked harder for
their money than the farmers did. He must
think of his old age. They wanted to take it
easy some day. He didn't want to find himself
with as little as Grandpa Stille had.

93

He kept on digging. He worked as hard as he had ever done, except that he had the boys to help.

The greatest change came when he bought the Ford. August had been one of those who kept his old horses as long as he could, but he had to come to the automobile, like the rest of the farmers. He went into "Wapsie" one Saturday and looked at cars. He had the agent take him out and teach him how to drive that afternoon, and he drove the car home at night. The family came out into the yard. The children shouted, "Mamma, see what pa's got!" August drove proudly, scowling, not sure whether he could miss all the buildings and stop where he wished. The boys ran up to ask excitedly, "Can you stop her, pa? Hey, look out for that wagon! Where'd you get her? How much was she?" After August went into the house they stayed out there, looking the little five-passenger car all over, testing the wheels, examining the engine.

"*Ja*, I s'pose they'll think it's theirs now," August grumbled.

Emma declared at first that she would never go in the car. Her timidity delighted all of them. The boys could take the auto; she would

94

drive with the horses and the old buggy.
"*Ach*," she said, "I don't trust those things.
You read about accidents all the time." "Well,
mamma, horses can run away, too. Old Dick
ran away with Frank." "*Ja*, but then——"
But the children teased her so much that she
finally consented to get into the car. "Now,
ain't this better than the old buggy?" the boys
demanded. "*Ja*, well it ain't so bad, I guess,"
was all that they could get her to say. She
never really liked the car. She was always
nervous and looking out for accidents. For
some reason she didn't believe that August could
learn to be a good driver. "*Ach*, it's so late for
him to learn!" She had never been afraid when
he had a hand on the reins when they had gone
out with the horses. After the boys learned to
drive, she liked it better. She said it seemed
more natural for young folks to learn things like
that. She had faith in Carl and Johnnie. But
when she went with August, she always kept one
hand on the seat ready to open the door and
jump out. And although he got to handle the
car in any kind of weather and on any kind of
roads, as all farmers did, August never did drive
as well as the boys. They could seem to get the

95

thing cranked when he couldn't. It was a knack they had. Emma noticed that he was ready to let them do the driving when he could.

The car meant that they could get away from the farm. They went into town oftener. They drove to Elva's and Frank's and Mollie's. The relationship nearly always had Sunday dinner together now. They went into church more regularly, and to other things in town—basketball games to see the boys play, the lecture course.

They even took a little trip, the first time they'd really been away from the farm. Once after harvest they left the boys to look after the farm, and August and Emma and Marguerite drove down to Turkey Creek and visited all of August's folks. The old man Kaetterhenry was dead, of course, but most of August's brothers and sisters were still living about there. It was a beautiful time of the year. The autumn was lovely there in the timber, among the hills. They all drove out for picnics together. They made plans with Sophie and her husband to drive to the "Picture Rocks" on the Mississippi some year, stopping at the little old town of Guttenberg, where their folks had stopped when they

96

came up the Mississippi and had bought their first farm implements.

Then the road past the farm, between Richland and "Wapsie," was made a highway. That dreadful hill by Ed Hunter's farm was graded down so that no one need be afraid of it any more. The old country road was widened and ditched and gravelled; the tall black-eyed Susans and the sweet clover were ruthlessly slashed down into dusty stubble. Although August fought the highway and joined other farmers in grumbling at the taxes, still "it made it handier." They went into "Wapsie" often, although they still did most of their trading in Richland, believing it must be cheaper there, since the stores had fewer goods and they were set out with less style.

That used to be a country road along which occasional wagons and buggies jolted. Now it was a gravelled highway, "Primary Road 5." Cars flashed down it all day, and on Sundays in the summer there was a constant stream of travel. Head-lights and wind-shields gave off sharp white flashes as cars whirred past on the light-coloured, glittering gravel. It was a wonder to Emma to sit on the porch on Sunday afternoons

97

and count how many vehicles went by. But grandpa wouldn't even try to count. "*Ach*, no! no! no!" was all that he would say. This was all so wicked on Sunday!

August had kept his hands on other things, but he couldn't keep the boys from using the car. When they took their girls, it wasn't an all-day occasion, as when Frank had got grandpa's old buggy to drive Lottie to the fair. They went out on Sunday afternoons when they felt like it. August would go out and find the car gone again. It was no use trying to stop them. Emma thought it dreadful for the boys to "pleasure-drive on Sunday," against which the Richland Methodist church was making a last futile stand, as against cards and dancing; but both she and August got used to it. All the young people seemed to do it. But one thing August said: if he ever heard of his boys driving to a Sunday base-ball game, they could never have the car again.

Grandpa never grew accustomed to all this. He was now too mild, too feeble and withdrawn, to protest much against it; but he would say sadly, when he saw that the boys were gone,

98

German. All the feeling that he had was naturally and instinctively on the side of Germany. But most of the farmers were agreed. "Well, they've got to fight it out among themselves. It's their business; 'tain't ours." That was the way that August felt. He went about his own business.

Grandpa was the one who got excited. The old man, so withdrawn, his inner life known now to no one but himself, buried in strange dreams and prayers and fervours, now suddenly came back to the world. It was as if all at once childhood things, which had long been buried, came surging to the surface and overwhelmed him with memories. He went back to his boyhood in that little village in Mecklenburg whose name the boys had never heard before. Now he was always talking about it—Gultberg. "*Ja*, in Gultberg den——" "Gultberg? What's that? What's he talking about?" the boys asked, half amused. This was all far away to them. It tickled them, they said, to see "grandpa get himself all worked up" over something he had painstakingly read in the paper; come tottering out from his room, in his old felt slippers and patched brown trousers, his dark, sunken eyes

101

burning, shaking one long, bony finger and pouring out a lot of broken English and German that they could only half understand. "Are de Germans so bad, den? *Mein* oldt *Vater*, *mein* Uncle Carl, I remember in de old country, were dey den all such bad men? No, no." They would listen, grinning a little, until he was exhausted and would go back to his room, shaking his head and mourning sadly, "*Ach*, no, *nein*," to sit in the old rocker, sadly, his hands in his lap, muttering as he used to do about the Sunday travel.

Emma tried to calm him; she was afraid that the excitement would hurt him. She couldn't see why he was so affected by this, by things so far away; but of course he was thinking about his old home.

But when this country went in, all this was changed. Then feelings that had never been known before were all about. Then the taunts, the talk about Huns and *Boche*, made farmers like August for the first time actually realize their German ancestry. August had always taken it for granted that he belonged in this country. They awoke a deep racial resentment that could not come flaring out into the open but

102

had to remain smouldering, and that joined with the fear of change, the resentment at interference, into a combination of angry feelings.

This centred chiefly in a deep opposition to the draft. To have someone tell his boys to do this and that! To take away his help on the farm just when he needed it most! To have somebody just step in and tell them where they had to go! Was that what happened in this country? Why had his people left the old country, then, if things were going to be just the same?

Carl was twenty-three now, Johnnie twenty. Carl's was among the first three names drawn in Richland, where he had to register. It was on the list in the post office—Carl Kaetterhenry, along with Ray Powers and Jay Bennett, the preacher's son. August stormed, wanted to know what right the Government had. But Carl took it quietly. There was no use kicking, he said. His name happened to be one drawn, and that was all there was to it.

What roused August to the greatest anger was that Harlan Boggs, the banker's son in "Wapsie," should get exempt, while his boy had to go. Harlan Boggs had appealed to the board

103

and got exemption on the grounds that he couldn't be spared from the bank because of Liberty-bond work. But it didn't matter to the board, August said, that he couldn't get help and that they should take his boy right in the midst of the harvest season. Johnnie was working for Frank that year, and Carl was the only one he had on the farm. They said, "Produce, produce," but how was he going to do it when he got no help? There was all this talk about the women working on the farms, but August didn't see many of those high-school girls from Richland coming out and offering to do his threshing for him. Where were all these women working, then?

Grandpa quieted down after he learned that this country was in the war; regarded with a hurt, sorrowing, bewildered wonder that it should be fighting Germany. That was all that mattered to him, all that he could see of it. Carl went in to say good-bye to him, embarrassed and a little afraid of what grandpa might do. The old man rose from his chair, holding it by one arm, and quietly shook Carl's hand. Then he returned to his solitary brooding. It was strange and remote, the touch of that dry, aged, bony hand, although grandpa had been there in the house ever since Carl could remember.

The train left in the early morning. August drove his family in, Emma and Carl and Marguerite. Johnnie and Frank and Frank's wife came in Frank's car; Mary and Elva and Roy in Roy's. There was a little group at the small wooden station: the other two boys and their families, a few people from town, one or two detached travelling men. The family stayed awkwardly in the depot, didn't know what to do or to say to one another. Johnnie and August went out to see if the train was in sight.

Just before the train came—the morning *Clipper*, the Chicago train, by which clocks were set and rising timed—old Jerry McGuire the postmaster, an old Catholic who had come into office when "the Democrats came in," lined the three boys up on the station platform and read the President's Proclamation to them. It was a strange, solemn, unreal scene. Even the people who saw it didn't believe in it. The three boys standing there, their figures against the dim red of the harvest sunrise, with solemn

105

blank faces, frowning a little to keep down any signs of emotion. One of the mothers sobbed. Emma wept only a little, effacing herself even now. Carl looked big and fresh between the other two boys, Jay Bennett, a thin boy, dissipated in a small-town way; Ray, gawky and sunburned, with a wild head of hair. Carl was such a big, sturdy boy! He had his father's fresh-coloured skin, only finer-grained, rough light hair, full boyish lips, and clear blue eyes.

The little town was silent. Away from the station stretched pastures, the dew lying wet and heavy on red clover and tall weeds. The train came bearing down upon them, puffing out blackish smoke into the pale morning sky. It went black and big into the red prairie-sunrise. The fields were left silent again. The scattered group of people on the platform got into their battered cars and drove back home to the morning chores.

When Johnnie had to go, they were more used to it.

It was a queer time at home. It was so strange to be without the boys! August was a big, vigorous man, but now he realized for the first time, now that he had everything to do alone,

106

that he was getting older. He had never
stopped working hard; but now he saw that,
strong and dogged as he was, he couldn't quite
do the work he had done in those days when they
first went on the farm. He didn't even think
of getting Emma out into the field now.
"Mamma" belonged in the house.

The feeling in the neighbourhood against the
German farmers had grown to a degree that
would have seemed incredible at the beginning
of the war. August "got off easy" compared
with some of them. He had two boys in the
service, he could keep his mouth shut, he bought
Liberty bonds, although he didn't like to be told
to do so. If it had not been for Carl and
Johnnie in the army, he might have refused, like
old Rudolph Haas, out of pure Kaetterhenry
stubbornness. It was the thought of Carl and
Johnnie that kept him from flaring up too
fiercely when the boys yelled at him, when he
drove into Richland, "Hey, Dutchy! Old
Dutchman! Old Dutchy Kaetterhenry!" Once
or twice he threatened, and started after them;
but usually he only glared at them, smothering
his impulse to fight. Some of the other German
farmers came up before the board because of

things they had said, or were reported to have said. Old Haas's corn-crib was burned. But nothing worse happened to August than being yelled at on the street and finding painted in crude red letters on his barn: "Old Dutchy Kaetterhenry. Hun. Bosh. Look Out."

They were having terrible times down around Turkey Creek, which was solidly German, and where there had been more resistance to the draft. One of August's brothers had been threatened. A mob of boys and men from "Wapsie" had gone down there one night and tarred and feathered the preacher at the old Turkey Creek German church.

August kept himself in hand because of the boys and because of the way Emma worried. And underneath all his anger was a strange, hurt, puzzled incredulity. Hadn't he lived here all his life, been born twenty miles from here? Didn't everybody know August Kaetterhenry? Hadn't he been a good farmer and citizen and church-member all his life? There was at the same time something fiercely real and yet utterly incredible about the whole thing.

Emma worried about the boys. She never heard the telephone ring that she didn't think it might be a message for them, as their neighbour, Mrs. Griffin, had got. She knew now that of all the children Johnnie was her boy, just as Carl was August's. Carl was steadier and more level-headed. She had a feeling that Carl would take care of himself, that nothing would happen to him. But Johnnie—he would go rushing into everything.

It was long since she had done the milking and all such work. Despite having less cooking and washing to do, it was hard on her. She was ailing more or less, although she kept up. That old trouble that she had sometimes had before came back on her. "Spells with her stomach," she called it. The family had long supposed that these spells were just something that mamma had, but now she told Mollie that August wanted to get the doctor out for her. She always said, "*Ach*, no. Wait awhile. I guess it won't last long." Then she would feel better again.

Things were strange all about these days. One of the queerest things that happened was Mary's marriage. Years ago Mary had gone with Joe Fields. He used to take her to the county fair when Roy took Elva. But then

109

Country People

Mary had wanted to go to school, and Joe had married Ada Griffin. He was a widower now, with four little children. Mary was "sewing around." People hadn't even known that Joe was "looking in that direction" again. But all at once he and Mary turned up at the Kaetter-henry farm married! Well, the family were glad that she was settled, although they didn't see how she was going to be strong enough to do all that work and look after those four children. But she and Joe, it seemed, had always liked each other, although once Mary had wanted a different kind of man from Joe. The family thought it was a good thing to have her settled down at last. This was something to write the boys, if it didn't take them so long to get their mail that it would be old before they heard of it.

Carl had gone into the army first, but Johnnie got across before he did. Carl had his father's knack with horses. They kept him down at one of the Southern camps training new recruits to handle the horses. Johnnie was in the machine-gun division. He was right in the thick of it, as they thought Johnnie would be sure to be. He was wounded once, but his family didn't hear of

Part Three

1: Operation

CARL's wife was a great help in the house. She was much like Carl himself, fresh-faced, light-haired, rather quiet, but good-tempered and sturdy and vigorous. At first Emma tried to treat her like company, but Clara said that she was used to doing things and really tried to take some of the hardest work off Emma's hands. Emma had always had the feeling that she must be responsible for all that was done in the house. But now she let Clara do things for her. She told the relatives she "liked Carl's wife real well. She was nice to have around."

The family thought that Emma might get to feeling better now that the boys were at home again and she didn't have all that worry. But she was still miserable. People noticed that she didn't look well; said, "Ain't you thinner than you been the last few years? What they been doing to you?" August was slow to

believe anything really wrong with any of his
family. But he did see that Emma didn't look
right.

Then she was "right down sick." August
didn't know when Emma had ever really given
out before, and it frightened him. He asked her
if she didn't want to try that place where Mary
had gone. The neighbours and relatives all
came in to help and advise. They all said
wisely that it was something that had better be
looked after. They told about Mrs. Ed Kohler.
None of these doctors could help her, and old
Bowen had said she was dying, until she had
gone up to the clinic at Rochester. Others had
gone there, as formerly they had tried patent
medicine and mud-baths. People talked Rochester, Rochester, until August asked Emma,
"Well, do you think you'd like to go up there,
then?" She said, as she always did, "*Ach*, I
don't know." But he could see that she rather
wanted to go. All the children urged it. They
wanted August to take her there. Carl and
Clara could look after the farm. Finally
August said he guessed he'd take her up there.

It was the greatest journey that they had ever
taken together. August had gone to Chicago

116

once with stock during the war, and when she was a little child Emma had come out to Iowa from New York with her parents; but they had never gone farther on the train together than to Dubuque, about thirty miles away.

Everyone knew that he was taking her to Rochester. People who had been there, or had had members of their family there, came over to tell Emma details of operations. When they saw that she was getting frightened they said, "Well, now, maybe you'll find it's just some little thing that don't need an operation, like Myrtie Rohrer."

It seemed to Emma and August that they were taking a terrible and final journey. Carl drove them to the station. They were taking Marguerite with them. Clara stood in the kitchen doorway, her arms hugged in her apron, because the March wind was cold. As Carl cranked the car and hurried around to the side to get in, she waved her arm and called, "Don't worry about your chickens." Emma asked fearfully, "What's that she said?" "Said not to worry about your chickens, mamma." They drove out through the deep, black, sticky mud of their own drive, out to the highway, with its

brown gravel gritty and wet in the sharp, windy
March air.

At the station they felt a faint importance and
pride when August told the people who inquired,
"*Ja*, I'm takin' her up to Rochester; see if those
fellows can't help her some a'ready."

The children, too, felt pride in the clipping
from the Richland *Banner* that they sent on to
the folks up at Rochester.

Mr. and Mrs. August Kaetterhenry left Tuesday
for Rochester, Minn., to consult the Drs. Mayo in re-
gard to her health. Mrs. Kaetterhenry has been in poor
health for some time, and it is hoped by her many
friends that she will find speedy relief at this famous
establishment."

The trip up to Minnesota, bleak and sharp as
the weather was, had interest for them. It was
almost the first time that they had been in any
other State than Iowa. August was in the
smoking-car. He came back and said to Emma
and Marguerite, "Do you know you're in Minnesota a'ready?" "Oh, are we?" Emma
looked out of the window. She thought with a
thrill, "We're in another State!" August kept
watching to see how the country looked, and

118

whether things were as far along up here as he
had left them back there. He saw some nice
farms, he said. But the land was flatter than
around home, and a fellow to whom he had been
talking told him that they had more wind up
here. August said he didn't think he'd like to
live where they were all Swedes and Norwegians.
He hadn't seen any farm yet that looked better
than his own in Richland Township.

They took the journey in the day coach and
thriftily ate the lunch that Clara and Lottie had
put up for them, taking the fried chicken out of
the pasteboard box and telling Marguerite to
brush the crumbs off the dusty, red plush seat.
They looked like country people, August heavy
and silent, his farmer's red neck showing rough
and creased above his collar in the back, in his
heavy coat and overshoes and cap; Emma subdued and uncertain over the journey, looking
with a kind of fearful curiosity at the other people in the train; a sickly woman with greyish
hair and old-fashioned glasses, in a stiff, black
velvet hat and an old black coat of some imita-
tion fur with old-fashioned sleeves gathered
slightly at the top, a black skirt that came down
to her rubbers, black golf mittens. Even Mar-

119

guerite looked a little coarse and sullen, with her blue knitted tam pulled down upon her bright fuzz of hair.

They went to a boarding-house where some of their neighbours had gone, one that was said to be clean and that didn't charge as much as some. It was just as good as anybody'd want, Mrs. Griffin had told them. It was snowing when they got there, as they wrote back to the children, and they trudged up through the dismal streets, with their left-over dingy snow, August carrying the two suit-cases that Carl and Johnnie had let them have. The boarding-house was an old-fashioned, brown frame-house close to the medical buildings. Marguerite shared a room with an excitable, talkative woman who took pride in being in Rochester for the fourth time. She told Marguerite all about her different doctors, saying happily, "I said when I come in, 'Well, doctor, you've got me back again, you see.' Dr. Barnard knew me right away. Well, he'd ought to; this is the fourth time I been in Rochester. He's had to examine me twice before his-self. He says, 'Well, Miss Parmenter, I see I have. What do you mean by this?' He's awful good-natured; not like some. Always a-jokin' you when you come in there."

The Kaetterhenrys had nothing to say to the other boarders at first. They ate in silence, asking one another in hushed voices for butter or bread. But they had to wait several days until they could have their turn at the clinic. One of the women who sat in the shabby boarding-house parlour, with its ancient furnishings, began to talk to Emma. "You here on your own account?" she said. "I thought you was the one. What's your trouble?" They talked over symptoms together. The woman told Emma what she must expect in going through the clinic, and terrified her with descriptions of all the tests that she herself had had to have, leaving out no detail. She thought that Emma must have just what her cousin's wife had had, and she had spent four months in the hospital and now was going to have to come again. At night Emma and August talked over the boarders together in their room, in hoarse whispers, Emma telling what she had gleaned of where this one lived, what that one's husband did, what was the matter with another one.

121

Country People

They started in at the clinic at last, when Emma was afraid that "mister would get restless and want to go home if they didn't get in pretty soon." When the girl at the desk asked them for what they had come, they said—looking at each other as if the other one might know —they didn't know, that was what they wanted to find out. She sent them patiently to the abdominal section, which was a good guess for most farmer people. Emma took the tests, while August stolidly waited in the lobby of the clinic building, with his overcoat thrown open and his cap on his knee. Emma wanted him around. He did not take an interest in watching the people, as she would have done, but he liked to see how the building was put up, to calculate how much space and how many rooms they must have and how many people there must have been going through it to-day.

He was just where Emma had left him. He said, "Well, what'd he tell you?" "*Ach*, I got to see another one to-morrow."

Gradually they felt themselves drawn into the life of the place. It was an experience to them, more than the mud-baths had been to Mary. Although they were bashful and ill at ease away

122

from home, it was not so hard getting acquainted
as they had thought. People talked to them—
the boarders, people who happened to sit near
them in the clinic—and wore away their country
shyness. Emma felt a kind of enjoyment in
talking over the tests she had taken, and the doctors she had seen, with three or four other people
who sat in the boarding-house parlour with the
landlady and talked. Her ailments had never
had any importance before. They always asked,
when she and August came in, "Well, still taking
tests?" "*Ja*, I guess that's what she'll always
be doing," August answered. Emma smiled
shyly. The boarders thought that that Mrs.
Kaetterhenry was a real sweet little person.
Even August fell into conversation with a fat
man who sat next him in the clinic and who was
also waiting for his wife. They talked about
their wives' illnesses, and the man told how the
crops had been in Wisconsin. August had some
conversation with a fellow from Texas that gave
him a travelled feeling. Marguerite went to the
movies and into the shops with Miss Parmenter,
who flew about town buying squares to make
drawn-thread handkerchiefs in the intervals of
examinations.

123

Country People

The strange and unaccustomed thing was the importance of Emma. August and Marguerite counted for nothing beside her here, were merely here to be with her. It was a new idea to both of them, and to Emma, too. August went in with her to the doctor who had examined her to hear the verdict. He did not make a murmur about the expense, although it was all so much more than he had figured on. Emma's value was strangely enhanced in his eyes when the doctor, a large, well-groomed, imposing man with a courteous manner that made Emma admire him, spoke respectfully of "Mrs. Kaetterhenry," outlined her condition, and said that she must go at once to the hospital.

The boarders all said, "Gall-bladder operation! Well, that's just what I thought from what she told me," although the woman who had thought that Emma had her cousin's wife's ailment was disappointed and unconvinced. This was a respectable and well-known operation, and it, too, seemed to raise Emma's value in some strange way. The boarders were interested, helped Marguerite to pack her mother's suit-case for the hospital, reassured, and condoled.

Emma seemed still more removed from their

common ways of life when she entered the hospital. August went into her room for a while, a small double room, Emma's bed across from another bed where a woman with a long, meager braid lay and talked in sepulchral whispers with a visitor in a hat with green plumes. Emma looked changed, in the narrow, white iron bed, so immaculate, different from their puffy featherbed at home, without her spectacles, her thin grey hair neatly parted and braided by the nurse. Both she and August felt a mysterious fear of "the sisters" who glided about the halls in their robes and rosaries. They had always felt a fascinated horror of the wickedness of the Catholics.

"It kind o' makes me creepy to have them around here," Emma protested.

"*Ach*, I guess they're all right. He wouldn't 'a' sent you here if they wasn't," August said.

All this whiteness and immaculateness seemed great splendour to them.

Emma had her operation the next day. August was really frightened then. The boarders all reassured him, all told of the wonders of the surgeon. August had seen him for a moment in the hospital—a short, plump, very clean man, exhaling a kind of unshakable vigour. August felt a tremendous awe of him. They both trusted him in the blind way that they trusted their Methodist God, because they must. It helped August, fed his pride, that his wife was to have a famous surgeon. But, although he said little, he was shaken. Emma had made him promise to be right there. It seemed now that August mattered more to her than Marguerite.

He waited in the sun parlour. He had never gone through such an endless morning. He tried to think about the farm, about what crops he would put in this summer; but under everything was a sinking, sickening dread in which he would suddenly be submerged. He was silent, turning his cap upon his knee. Marguerite sat restlessly beside him. She could not keep her hands still, fingered her dress and her beads and her hand-kerchief. People were wheeled past from the operating-room—mounds of white, some silent, some moaning. August looked at his watch. He went through terror. It shouldn't have taken as long as this. Something must have gone wrong. He tiptoed down the hall to Emma's room. Her bed was still empty.

The nurse came for them at last. They went,

solemn, shaken, on tiptoe, into Emma's room.
They felt awed, taken aback, at the sight of her
strange, pinched, colourless face at which they
stood awkwardly gazing.

"You can speak to her," the nurse said encouragingly. August was terribly in awe of Emma.
He did not know what to say.

"Well, it's over," he said finally.

"*Ja*, I guess so," Emma whispered.

Marguerite stood looking sullen and angry in
her fright. She hardly dared go near her mother,
kissed her quickly, barely touching her cheek,
when the nurse said that she might. They
stared awhile longer, tiptoed out.

The excitement of the day died down. The
boarders all said, "Well, she got through it all
right, I see. Sure. I knew she would. Well,
now you must telegraph the folks at home. I
expect there'll be some pretty anxious folks."

It was the first telegram that August had ever
sent. "Operation over mamma doing fine."
That, too, gave him importance.

After that August and Marguerite went twice
a day to the hospital in the motor-bus that
ploughed clumsily through the spring mud.
August always felt big and awkward and out of

127

place in that silent building, but he got to know
the faint odour of drugs.   He recognized some
of the people who always went up in the elevator
with him and felt a kind of kinship with them.
He even felt less awe of the gliding sisters.   He
wasn't dreadfully abashed now at the woman in
the other bed, who talked to him and Emma,
called him Mr. Kaetterhenry.

Emma now seemed to belong to the place.
She said that they were nice to her.   She took
with shy gratitude the first attention and petting
that she had had since she was a girl, with a kind
of feeling that she, a married woman and mother,
shouldn't have it, but a feminine pleasure in it.
The nurses liked her.   They were good to her,
petted and cared for her in a way that made Marguerite look at them wide-eyed, remembering that
this was mamma.   It was so strange to see
mamma waited on and of first importance!   The
other woman in the room was fretful and exacting.   Emma was such a contrast to her that the
nurses appreciated her all the more.   They told
her she mustn't be afraid to ask for what she
wanted, and they liked her shyness and fear of
giving them trouble.

For the first time Emma had a life in which

family were outsiders. She had a kind of intimacy with the nurses, and with the very spruce, black-haired young intern who came in and jested with her in a kind of fond teasing way that greatly flattered her. He never did learn how to pronounce her name, and called her blithely "Mrs. Katterhenry," at which she was to shy to protest.

As Emma grew better and his fright died down, poor August hardly knew what to do with himself. He never had been without work before in his life. He had never had a real vacation from the farm except that drive down into the Turkey timber, and then he had had the car to look after and had still talked crops with his brothers. When he could not be at the hospital, he hung about the boarding-house, yawned, sat drearily while the others were gossiping. He had never been a talker. He couldn't find the interest in the discussion of ailments that the others did, since he had never had any of his own. Now that he knew what it was, that Emma was getting better, he was no longer interested. There was no one just now to talk crops with him. That was the longest three weeks he had ever spent. He would rather have

129

been threshing. The boarders said, "Well, I expect you're getting anxious to get back to your work now, Mr. Kaetterhenry." He said, *ja*, he was. He worried about how Carl was managing the farm. He would have gone back if Emma hadn't begged him to stay.

The boarders said encouragingly, when they saw his restlessness, "Oh, the vacation'll do you good." "*Ja*, but I've had about enough of it, though," he said.

Emma, too, said that she was anxious to get back home, but in a way she was having the best time that she had had for years. She was taking her leisure with a clear conscience. She had never been treated with such consideration. She really hated to leave the nurses and the young intern.

When she got back to the boarding-house most of the boarders who had been there before her operation were gone. Miss Parmenter had left much disappointed because they had told her that she didn't need an operation; a little medicine was enough. Dr. Barnard had gone down in her estimation. Emma missed the care and attention which had embarrassed her so at first. She missed the visits of the young intern, with his flattering jests. The boarding-house seemed dreary.

The specialist at the clinic had a talk with August before they left for home. August listened, subdued and respectful. The doctor said that he "anticipated no trouble," but that Mrs. Kaetterhenry must do no heavy work this summer and must take things very easily. August heard him uneasily, agreed, "*Ja*, I guess we can manage that." Something in it appealed to his sturdiness and reliability, his feeling of protection. Down underneath was a little feeling of bewildered guilt. This thing had opened August's eyes a little.

They went back to Richland feeling journeyed and full of Rochester. August was glad to get back to the farm and plunged at once into the late spring work. Emma was fearful of her strength at first. She remembered the admonitions. Clara said, "Now, mamma, we mustn't let you overdo." But when Emma got home, into the familiar routine, she threw off invalid ways. She had always worked here. They couldn't keep her from doing things. No one knew the people of whom she talked in Rochester. The surgeon, the doctors, meant nothing to

131

Clara and Carl. The event of her home-coming was soon over. She settled down into the old ways again. She didn't go around telling everyone of her operation, as Mrs. Griffin had done, but the experience stayed, sharp and momentous, in her mind.

August, too, was a little different. He seemed to accept with relief her settling back into the rôle of mamma. But he was more thoughtful of her. He asked her if she couldn't let Clara do this or that. He saw, they all saw, that she wasn't equal to the things that she used to do.

August had worried about the farm. But when he came back to it he couldn't find anything very wrong with Carl's management. Things seemed to look as usual. That summer Carl kept on with some of the things that he had been doing that August had never entrusted to any of the boys before.

Those years of the war, when he had had everything to do, had tired August. He had always intended to retire, take it easy, when he could afford it; but all these things brought him to it now. He announced to Emma one day that they might move in to town and leave the farm to Carl.

II: Town

THE chief question was what they should do with grandpa if they left the farm. He had lived in that little room so long! He was over eighty now. It would be hard for him to make any change. He wouldn't want to go to town with them; he was used to the country. Clara and Carl said, "Let him stay here," but Emma hated to do that. He was getting so old now and might need a good deal of care before long; and they were young people, and didn't want to be tied to the place. Grandpa ought to have some of his own children to look after him. August thought that Herman and Mollie ought to take care of him now. They had let Emma have the whole care of both grandma and grandpa always. Now it wouldn't hurt Mollie to do something for her father. The old man would be no expense to them. He had a tiny income from bits of his land that had been left to him, enough to buy tobacco for him and *Die Flammende Fackel*, and the few clothes and things that he needed. Now August and Emma were going into town to take it easy. Emma wasn't going to be saddled with the care of grandpa, August said, as she had been with grandma.

They took grandpa's belongings over to Mollie's one day in the motor-truck that Johnnie had assembled from an old engine and various miscellaneous parts: the ancient rope-bed with the feather-mattresses, the two wooden rocking-chairs, the commode and little old mirror, the air-tight stove, the ancient, faded books. Mollie and Herman made little trouble about taking him. They would probably not move off the farm for years yet. They couldn't afford it. Herman hadn't done as well as August had. The Klauses had taken things more easily all along, were more happy-go-lucky and not such workers as the Kaetterhenrys. They were easy-going people, Herman a little, lean man with kindly, childlike eyes and a kind of innocence of speech, Mollie short and fat and shapeless, waddling, good-hearted. Their farm had a dingy old-fashioned house set close to a scraggly, tangled willow grove where the ground seldom

got a chance to dry and the blackbirds were
noisy. They used a gasolene engine for some of
their work, but they had no silo, no lights, and
only the old red-painted barn. Farm implements stood about the worn, grassless farm-yard.
August had always despised Herman a little for
being so easy-going and not getting anywhere.
They put grandpa's things into their own downstairs bedroom, moving up themselves into the
room that Ernie, their son, had had, and saying,
"*Ach*, we don't care. We can get along
anywhere."

Emma felt a dreadful sense of guilt and
desertion in leaving her father there. Not that
Herman and Mollie wouldn't be good to him.
But she knew how things went at Mollie's. It
didn't seem right to have him anywhere but in
that room where he had lived so long. But
August said it would have to be that way.

The Kaetterhenrys moved to town in the late
fall. There was no house that they could get
to rent. They had to take rooms in old Mrs.
Freeman's house until they could get a place of
their own. Houses were scarce in Richland,
where little business was done. This was a small
house in the south part of town, the old and

135

hilly part beyond the railroad tracks. It was half-frame, half-brick, painted a cream-yellow. They lived in the brick half. There were three rooms. They did their cooking and eating in one, August and Emma slept in another, and Marguerite had a cot and dresser in the third, which was their sitting-room. The rooms had the old square, small-paned windows, close to which some oak-trees rustled dry leaves. They had to get all their water from the pump next door. They had a stove only in the room where Marguerite slept, except the little oil-burner in the kitchen.

Emma didn't know just what August intended to do, whether he meant to buy or to build a house of his own. He still kept all such things to himself. He managed all the money. Once Johnnie said to her when he came over, "Heard pa was trying to buy one of those lots over by Cunningham's." "*Ach*, is he?" she said. "*Ja*, he don't tell me nothing." She did not think of making a fuss, as some would have done, but no one suspected the resentment that lay deep under her silence.

The children all said cheerfully, "Well, mamma, you can take it easy this winter. You

136

ain't got much to do here." She said a little complainingly, "No, I should say I ain't. I wish I had a little more." These three small rooms were nothing after she had locked after a farm-house. Of course there were the meals to get, and they were hard to cook on this little three-burner oil-stove, when she was used to her big range. Johnnie ate with them, although they didn't have room for him to stay there.

But she had all afternoon to herself and she hardly knew what to do. It was a long, snowy winter. There were not many side-walks in this part of town, and it was hard to get out anywhere. She didn't see the children as often as she had in the country. She didn't get out to Mary's once all winter. She knew a few people in town—her two sisters-in-law, Mrs. Henry and Mrs. Willie Stille—but this was too far for them to come and see her much. She had a cold, and didn't even get to church most of the winter.

Once she said to August:

"Johnnie says you're buying one of them lots over north."

"*Ja*, I guess maybe," he admitted.

"Well, are we going to build?"

"I guess we better build. They ain't no good

houses for sale. Why, don't you want to build?" he demanded.

"*Ach*, I'd like it, I guess. I just wondered what you was doing."

He grunted. But she had to find out from the children that he had actually bought a lot and that he was ordering lumber from the Great Western Lumber-yard. Elva demanded angrily, "Why don't pa ask you something about it? You ought to have some say-so about your own house, I should think. I'd like to see Roy do that." She said, "*Ach*, that's the way he always does." He did mean to let her have something to say about the way the house should be built, but buying the lot and things like that—he couldn't see how they concerned her. The house did, of course. She often wondered how much he had to pay for the lot, but she never asked him.

August's interest was all in the new house now. It was something to build up, as he had built up the farm. There were some pictures of houses in the window of the bank, a large card showing four of them, all planned by the same company, all more or less on the bungalow type. August went in several times to look at them. The banker always said, "Sure! Any of those appeal

138

to you, Mr. Kaetterhenry?" August replied cautiously, "*Ach*, I don't know. I ain't quite ready to build yet a'ready." "No, no. Well, they're pretty nice little houses." "*Ja*, they're pretty nice all right."

When he had got his mind pretty well made up, he asked for one of the sheets with the pictures and took it home to show to Emma.

"How'd you like to live in one of those?" he asked. He had always had a kind of idea that when he came to town he would put up a big house, one like Mr. Nixon's, the banker's, that had a porch all the way around. But it seemed that they weren't putting up many of those houses now. Mr. Nixon sent the contractor, Herb Carter, to see them. "Heard you folks were thinking some of building." Herb tried to get them to put up a pebble-dashed bungalow, like the one he had put up for Dan Myers the summer before. But they wouldn't agree to that. Emma wanted an upstairs. August wasn't sure that he liked this pebble-dash. It was a pretty new thing, and he wasn't sure how it would "hold." They compromised on a kind of semi-cottage with no attic and three small upstairs rooms.

139

Country People

That was a good part of town where their lot was. It was where the building would be going on now. The banker's son, Clarence Nixon, owned the lot next to theirs, they had heard. He would probably build as soon as he got married. There was no house so far on their side of the street except Tom Cunningham's, on the corner, and that faced the other street. There were no trees either—just a short, vacant block, beyond which were pastures.

They began work on the house as soon as they could in the spring. Herb Carter had a lot of houses to build. He always promised more than he could do. But they got along because August did so much of the work himself. He got a wagon and team from the boys and hauled his own sand and earth for the yard. He was a pretty good carpenter, handy, as many Germans are, and he helped with the lathing and siding. It kept the men on the job, too, to have him there. There wasn't much fooling with August Kaetterhenry, as people who had had to deal with him knew. He meant to have the house ready, so that they could move into it before winter.

The boys said laughingly, "Thought pa was

going to town to take it easy. He's working as
hard as he did on the farm. I'd want to be paid
good and plenty before I'd take to hauling all
that dirt."

But August liked it. The house filled up the
blank left by the farm. It fed his pride to be
putting up a good house, showing people that
he could afford it. There was the thought
that he had worked hard for this, that he
owed most of it to himself. People said, "You
always see Mr. Kaetterhenry going back and forth
from his new house. It must be going up pretty
fast. They say it's going to be nice."

It was up now, although the finishing wasn't
done inside. The *Banner* had an item about it:

"Mr. August Kaetterhenry has put up his fine new
house in the north part of town and is about ready for
the finishing. Mr. Kaetterhenry says that the first of
October will see them established in the new house."

He went over to see it in the early summer
evening, to take some more boards over, so that
the men would have them there in the morning,
but really to see how the place looked when he
wasn't working on it.

The house stood, new, bare, bright, on the raw

earth that was littered over with boards, shavings, pails of dirtyish mortar. It had had its first coat of paint, the upper story yellow, and the lower white. The shingles looked brown and fresh and had a woody smell. The porch roof sloped, and there was one of those dormer-windows in the centre that looked as if it had slipped down half-way. Narrow planks that bent a little led up over the porch steps and to the shining front door. The door was locked now. The house was past the stage when little girls could go in and find shaving-curls to hang over their hair, and when women could go there looking around and speculating on which room was which.

Inside, the house was new, echoing, still. The unstained floors and woodwork made August feel that he shouldn't be stepping about in his heavy shoes. The walls were rough, white, untinted. The bath-room was finished, although chunks of plaster lay around. He was proud of the shining pipes, the white porcelain of the fixtures still unwashed, with labels sticking to it. Another thing that he admired was the colonnade between the dining-room and living-room. It seemed queer to both of them not to have a parlour, but that was the way that houses were being made now. Although he had worked on this house, August could hardly believe in it, somehow, and that he was ever going to live here.

There were some small boards laid over the stairs to keep them clean. He thought he'd go up and see how it looked up there. But he did not stay long. It was dim up there, more silent, and his shoes made a fearful noise as he creaked from room to room. He had a stealthy feeling, as if someone would catch him there. These rooms kept the heat of the day. He was proud of the shining bronze-and-black registers in the walls.

Well, he guessed there was nothing he could do in here. He'd seen it all often enough.

He went outside. In the early summer evening there was a kind of sadness and bareness in the new house, standing stark against the pale evening sky, the new boards around, the raw dirt, the tools thrown down whenever the men had happened to drop them, the vacant lots beyond, and then the pastures stretching away, damp and fresh with dew, and the slow-moving forms of cattle.

They had wanted to move in in September, but

143

it was the middle of October before they could. Then the woodwork was all stained and varnished—light, shining golden-oak. They had had the walls in the front room "tiffanied." In the other rooms the walls were tinted light green or blue, with stencilled borders. They had bought new rugs for the two front rooms, with bright mottled patterns, and had had the old rag rugs made up into strips for the bedrooms. They were "doing everything right."

They hadn't brought in all of their furniture. August said some of it wasn't worth carting. The combination desk and bookcase, their bedroom furniture, the standard rocker, and three or four others—all these they had. The old rockers and the little old stand they put upstairs. Grandpa's old German Bible and the album and other old things went into the small store-room at the head of the stairs. Downstairs, as people said admiringly, half the things were new. The dining-room furniture was all new—a round table and four chairs with leather seats. They had kept some of the old chairs to help out when they had company. They had a new set of dishes, too, although they themselves used the old ones. The new ones were white, with scalloped

144

edges and a thin gold line. The dining-room table remained immaculate, or it a round, embroidered crash doily and a plant. They would do their eating in the kitchen. In the living-room was the piece of furniture that the children admired—a large brown davenport upholstered in stiff half-leather.

People went in to see the Kaetterhenrys. They said they were "fixed real nice."

At first it seemed queer to the children to see ma and pa in this brand-new modern house, with the shining floors and white plumbing and new furniture. But they got used to it quickly. Now, when they came into town, it was a settled thing that they should go to the folks' for dinner, and leave the babies there while they did their buying. They came in on Sundays to church, and all ate in the new dining-room, the daughters holding babies on their laps.

There was one thing that disappointed them, Emma especially. They had fixed up such a nice room for Johnnie and had thought that they could have him with them again. He had been rooming over in an old house near the garage. But just before they moved into the new house, he had driven over to "Wapsie" one day with his

145

landlady's daughter, and had come back and
announced himself married. Emma felt dreadfully, both because of the girl he had married
and because he hadn't told her and his father
about it.

They hated to think of his marrying "such a
little flip," as people in town called her. The
other two boys had married good workers, good
sensible girls, although in some ways they didn't
care much for Frank's wife. This Bernice was
only a junior in high school, a silly, rather pretty
girl, with a large, soft, powdered face and great
buns of dark hair showing the rats, melting,
foolish brown eyes. She wore sleazy over-
blouses moulded by her large, soft breasts, and
knee-skirts showing her fat white legs in cheap,
thin silk stockings that had a brownish cast.
She didn't know how to do anything. She and
Johnnie were to stay with mamma.

If Frank had married a girl like that, August
might not have forgiven him for years. He did
storm and say that he wouldn't do anything more
for Johnnie. But, although the marriage was
known as a great disappointment to the Kaetterhenrys, August's anger didn't last. In a way
this crazy action of Johnnie's, while it hurt

146

August, partly satisfied his old grudge about the way he had been treated in war-time, the peremptoriness of the Government in taking his boys off the farm, being called "Old Dutchy Kaetterhenry." If Johnnie had not gone to war, he would never have done such a thing. He had not been the same boy since, as anyone could see.

Johnnie quarrelled with Bernice's mother, an old Tartar, and he and Bernice went to live in some rooms up over the hardware store. Their baby was born soon after that. Women whispered how long it should have been before the baby ought to have come. But Junior was the prettiest, sturdiest, fattest baby in the relationship. It gave Emma something to do to go over to Johnnie's rooms and clean up and help Bernice with the baby.

Johnnie seemed to be settling down now. Being older than Bernice made him seem older and more staid to himself. August said that if he had really made up his mind now to stay in the garage business, and not just tinker, they'd see what they could do for him.

147

Part Four

I: Retired Farmers

PEOPLE asked the children now:
"Well, how do the folks like it in town?"

"Oh, pretty good, I guess," the children answered. "Mamma likes it a lot better since they're in their new house. I guess pa kind o' misses the farm, though."

"I guess Marguerite's glad they've moved in."

"Oh, sure, *she's* glad. It suits her just fine."

The Kaetterhenrys were settled in town now, retired farmers.

Marguerite was the one who had profited by the change. She was a town girl now. Her sisters said that she acted as if she had never lived in the country. She was in high school now, where she played basket-ball and went around with the girls. Marguerite Kaetterhenry was a good-looking girl. She was tall, large-boned, but still thin, with a fresh skin that was apt to break out a little. Her fuzz of bright

151

light hair she wore in huge side-puffs. She was very particular about how her clothes should be made. She wouldn't buy shoes at one of the general stores in Richland, but made her father take her in to "Wapsie," or went to Dubuque with one of the boys when they were going. She was popular in high school, had good marks in her studies, and went to all the parties, although the Kaetterhenrys wouldn't let her go to the town dances in the opera-house. But she was a kind of stranger at home.

She did not look as if she belonged to the same tribe as her sisters, when they came to town. Mary lived away out in the country, near the old mill. She looked aged and hollow-eyed, with dark skin and those glowing, shy, intelligent dark eyes. Her clothes were shabbier than her mother's. Elva took more pains with hers. She still had her white skin, but somehow her things had a country look. She was getting fat and matronly and sloppy, with all those fat white babies of hers. Clara, of course, was young and fresh-looking, and she looked well in the clean ready-made bungalow aprons that she wore out on the farm. But when she came to town, she seemed different, coarser, and she wore

shabby, high black shoes with her thin summer
dresses. Lottie, Frank's wife, was a heavy,
coarse, homely woman, with straight red hair
and a thick-freckled face. Marguerite would
never be satisfied with what her sisters had had.

In some ways the Kaetterhenrys lived much as
they had done on the farm. They did most of
their living in the kitchen. August always
washed his hands and face there, at the sink, in
the granite basin, instead of in the bath-room;
and he kept an old pinkish comb and his shaving-
things on the shelf above the sink. They used
their old dishes and ate from the oilcloth.

They had arranged to get their cream and eggs
from the farm, but they found that it was very
different from having those things right at hand
in abundance. Emma said that she had to learn
to cook all over again. They were sparing of
milk and butter when they had to pay for these
things in cash. They got several quarters of
meat when Carl butchered, and Emma put it up
in jars, as she had always done. But somehow,
when they were so near town, they found themselves getting more fresh meat. Emma canned
quarts and quarts of vegetables, too. The cellar
was full. They couldn't use half the things.

153

They couldn't have chickens because they might dig up the lawn, which was freshly seeded.

August had let Carl keep the old car and had bought a new sedan. They drove a little more now, oftener to "Wapsie" and to Dubuque, where they got into the habit of doing their important shopping, like most Richland people. But August used the car chiefly for going back and forth to the farm. He wouldn't let Marguerite drive it, and of course Emma never thought of doing so. They still did little pleasure-driving. They took out the minister and his wife for a drive, went two or three times to Turkey Creek. In the hot summer evenings the car was locked in the garage, although they might have been out getting the freshness from the open country, where ghostly vapour rose from the cornfields and the trees looked misty and drenched in the loneliness of evening.

They got considerable consolation from the church. Now they were among the chief and faithful members. If the Kaetterhenrys were not in their pew, the minister knew that something was wrong with them, and took pains to call the next week. They were among the eight or nine who attended the prayer-meetings.

154

Emma had a kind of fondness and loyalty for the church because of her father, and August remembered it as the best thing in his young days. Going to church, and being steady and a good worker, and not drinking, and paying his bills, and saving money, were all part of the same thing. August and Emma still attended the Hon. Mr. Bossingham's Bible class, where August sat dumb and Emma occasionally made a timid answer. They never said much at church-meetings, but they could always be counted upon to be there. After the evangelist had been to Richland—a modern evangelist who had a singer who shouted, "Now put a little pep into these hymns, people!" not like the old travelling evangelists who used to go around to the camp-meetings—they offered the use of their house for one of the cottage prayer-meetings that were held for as long as a month before they petered out.

But although the church was still a social and business centre in a little country town like Richland, one doctor attending the Methodist church, the other the Congregational, it didn't seem to have the importance that it had had when they were young people in the country here. The

155

children didn't make the effort to come in to services that they had made, easy as it was for them now, compared with those old days of buggies and dirt roads. There were too many other places where people could go now. August and Emma made Marguerite go to church and Sunday school, but after the League she went walking, on pleasant nights, with her current admirer.

And, really, it was only as a kind of deep-rooted custom, a bulwark against worrying changes, an idea, that August cared for the church. He often went to sleep during the services. He did not get the sentimental and emotional satisfaction out of the prayers and sermons and hymns that Emma did. It did not fill the same place in his life. He had never questioned anything, but it was doubtful what these things really meant to him.

Emma was getting used to town. As the children said, she liked it better now that they were in their own house. She was still very quiet, but she was beginning to go about a little more than formerly. Her sister-in-law, Mrs. Henry Stille, "got her into" the Social Circle Club, a collection of elderly ladies who met every

Tuesday to eat and talk. They had no program, like the Tourist Club, took up no "line of study." The club was only and frankly for social purposes. The *Banner* said of it:

"The Social Circle Club held its weekly meeting on Tuesday last at the pleasant new residence of Mrs. August Kaetterhenry. The ladies brought fancy work and, after a pleasant hour spent in social intercourse, were served with a delicious luncheon by the hostess, after which the club adjourned, thanking the hostess one and all for a delightful afternoon's entertainment."

Then there was the Aid Society. This, too, was composed largely of the older women of the church, who were still willing to get up big suppers, work at cleaning the church, make sheets and pillow-cases for the missions that they supported, and raise money for the parsonage fund by making quilts which women from "Wapsie" came down to buy. Emma enjoyed these quilting-afternoons in the quiet, chilly church basement, to which she went with Mrs. Willie Stille, with all the women sitting about in old-fashioned comfort, talking over neighbour-hood affairs, telling what their husbands and children had done, as they worked together at

157

the big quilting-frame. It was like her girl-hood days, when she was getting ready to be married, and they had held quilting-bees in the country. There was the crisp smell of coffee, which some of the ladies were getting ready on the oil-stove, coming in and saying, "Well, don't you ladies think you better quit working so hard and have a little coffee for a change?" She helped at the church suppers, was one of those who could be counted upon to work in the kitchen. But it was noticed that the Kaetter-henrys were always careful not to donate too much.

Emma still had the feeling that August mustn't be kept waiting a minute for his meals and that she "must be getting back."

She took more pains with the house than she had ever taken with the one in the country. It was all so bright and shining, and she wanted to keep it that way. Marguerite, of course, didn't get things out of order as the boys had done. Emma raised plants, geraniums, and coloured foliage, and a sword-fern for the front window that she hoped would grow huge, like Mrs. Henry Stille's. She did more sewing than she had done before. She used to count on Mary for that, but Mary had less time than she did now. Emma made Marguerite's clothes, under minute and fretful and exacting directions. "No, mamma, I told you I had to have the belt *down* lower. This makes me look like Lottie." She got patterns from other women and crocheted wide elaborate yokes for Marguerite's corset-covers and camisoles.

She took care of the grandchildren when the young people wanted to go somewhere. She went out into the country to help out when there was sickness at the homes of any of the children. She missed the farm sometimes—missed the quiet, her work with the poultry, the feeling of the old rooms, the country air and sounds. But she kept busy enough.

August was the one who felt that he had nothing to do. The house was finished now. Life moved along, and what else was there to do? He was taking it easy now. He made a kind of religion of the garden and the lawn. He looked forward to the meetings of the stockholders of the Farmers' Bank, in which he had an interest. He made a rite of going downtown for the mail and the meat. But all this meant nothing.

159

There was no club for him. For some obscure reason he "didn't believe in lodges." He paid his subscription to the church, and that was the end of it. He read the Richland *Banner* and a Dubuque paper and a farm journal. He cared for nothing else. There was no library in Richland, no place where magazines were sold, but he would not have patronized such places if he had had them, although Emma might have done so.

He didn't come right home when he went down for the mail. He got into the habit of hanging around with the other retired farmers, in at Dawson's store or at the post office. Not at the barber-shop. The "tougher element" hung out there, and at the restaurant, which had a pool hall in connection. The men talked a little about politics, but mostly about farms changing hands, and crops and roads, with minute observations on the weather.

"Well, that was just about a frost we had last night."

"Yeh. Little too windy for a frost."

"My wife thought some of her plants had been frosted."

"No. Wasn't quite a frost. Our plants didn't show any sign of it."

Most of them had a kind of seedy look. They walked heavily, without spring. They didn't know what to do with themselves.

People said, "Have you noticed how old Mr. Kaetterhenry's getting to look? He don't seem like the same man he did when they first moved into town. I wonder if he can be well." He wasn't very well. He had headaches, trouble with his stomach, once a dizzy spell. He was eating the same heavy meals that he had eaten when he was working hard on the farm, coffee and meat three times a day. August thought he had to have his meat.

It was true that all at once he was beginning to show his age. Emma looked no older now than he did. She had gained flesh again since her operation, and some of the lines had gone from her face. August, when he decided to retire, had been a hearty, vigorous man seemingly in the prime of life. But now all at once his old colour was gone, his shoulders were slack, his vigorously bright curling hair was sparse and faded, and he walked like a man ten years older. He actually looked older than Herman Klaus, who had always been a little dried-up fellow. August had never had anything the matter with

161

him except when he had lost two fingers from his left hand in the corn-shredder. But now he began buying a patent tonic at the drug-store, and he and Emma both took it.

Emma said that she believed half the trouble was that August had nothing to keep him busy any more. He did a little hauling. There was a job vacant in the lumber-yard. He would have liked to take it, at seventy dollars a month, but his old stubbornness kept him from it. He had said that he wanted to quit work. Actually he would have been glad at times to work on the roads or the section. But no work was vital any more. No work looked forward to anything. He didn't want someone else for his boss. Everything that he had done had been for the farm. The farm had always come first. He had always talked about retiring some day, quit this slaving; but he had never really looked forward to it. He had used every energy to build up the farm. He had done it, from almost nothing, by his own efforts, and now that he had made a fine place of it, Carl was living on it and he had moved to town. Well, that was what everybody did. He would not have wanted to be like Herman, not able to do it.

The boys had speculated upon whether pa
would be able to stay away from the farm.
They weren't surprised to see him going out
there. He made excuses at first. When he got
the new sedan, he drove out just to see what Carl
was doing. Then he said, "Want me to help
you some with that ploughing?" Then he
began to go regularly, except when the weather
was too bad and he was forced to hang about
the house, looking at the farm journal and trying
to take a nap.

He and Emma had always thought of taking
a trip, but it seemed now that neither of them
really wanted to go.

The farm looked different now, more so as
time went on. When August and Emma sometimes drove out there for Sunday dinner, it gave
them a kind of shock when they turned into the
drive. The place was theirs, and yet it wasn't.
The house was different. Carl and Clara were
getting new furniture. They used grandpa's old
room for a store-room. They didn't like the
upstairs, which was not well finished. They had
a brass bed and a shiny mail-order dresser in the
downstairs bedroom, which was full of the baby's
things, thrown around everywhere. They had

a new bright-coloured rug in the parlour, where there was none of the old furniture except the organ, which Marguerite had refused to have moved into town. Clara said she didn't know why they kept it there, since neither of them could play a note. She wanted a Victrola if crops were good this year. Carl had made a little cage for the baby, like one that they had seen in a store window in Dubuque. They let him play there on the new parlour rug, with all his celluloid animals and the little doll like one of the characters in the funny papers. None of Emma's children had ever been permitted to be in the parlour.

It was still different out on the place. August thought that Carl was doing a good deal of experimenting with new things. August had never believed in sweet clover for pasturage. He called sweet clover a weed. Now Carl had got a lot of new seed from the state agricultural college. August couldn't get used to the feeling that he couldn't tell Carl just what to do. Carl was the boss now. He was good-tempered, didn't say much. But August noticed that he kept on with exactly what he had planned to do. He was a Kaetterhenry. August worked on the farm, but then what did that mean when he was no longer doing it for anything? The life had gone out of his work. Sometimes he hated to go out there, although he couldn't stay away.

Carl didn't like to have him come, either, as he told Frank. Pa was too used to thinking he could do anything he pleased there. They had quarrels once or twice.

Emma, all of them, thought that August was working too hard. They said, "You don't need to go out to that farm and kill yourself." He kept on stubbornly. One day he was overcome with the heat out there. Carl had to bring him home in the sedan. But even after that he wouldn't stop. Carl had to be careful, and scheme so that his father would get the easier part of the work.

"Mr. Kaetterhenry looks real bad," people said. He would not admit it. Emma wanted him to try this and that that other people recommended. The children said, "Pa'll have a stroke some day if he isn't careful."

He was never so vigorous again after that heat prostration. He knew that he was sick, but he tried obstinately not to give in, to hang on. Then one day, coming home from town, he had
165

a kind of dizzy spell. He got home all right, and no one knew it. But it frightened him. It broke his resistance. He told Emma that he believed there was something the matter with him. The next day Emma telephoned the children that she and pa were going to Rochester again.

II: Obituary

IT was in the dead of winter that August and Emma took their second trip to Rochester. They did not take Marguerite with them this time. She was going to stay with her uncle Henry Stille, so that she needn't miss school. Altogether the trip seemed less eventful than the first one that they had made, when everything was new.

August was not interested in the farms this time, or the country. It lay under a heavy crust of snow, the willow-trees pencilled bleak and small upon a grey sky. Although they had both had such awe of the operation before, this time there was a different fear in their hearts, down under everything, gnawing in silence.

They went to their same old boarding-house. The landlady did not recognize them until they told their names and reminded her of when they had been here before. Then she exclaimed:

"Oh, my! Well, I should say! Well, what

are you folks back here for? Are you the sick
one this time, Mr. Kaetterhenry? Missus looks
fine, though."

They did not like the place so well as before.
They were used to the shining immaculateness
and comforts of their new house now. The bedroom, the dining-room, with the brown linoleum
and the little step up from the ancient parlour,
seemed darker and shabbier to them. They did
not know any of these boarders. Somehow, it
seemed to them that they must meet some of
those who had been here before, that they must
belong to the boarding-house.

The landlady tried to cheer them. She said:
"Oh, they'll fix you up over there. They're
great folks. Not much them doctors can't do."

Emma said:

"*Ja*, if he'll do what they say."

"Oh, he will. That's what he's come here
for." She rallied him: "I never thought I'd see
you folks here on your account, Mr. Kaetterhenry. Ain't you ashamed of yourself? My,
I remember that Mrs. Boohey that was here with
her husband, had the operation on the jaw, used
to say, if her husband looked half as strong as

Mr. Kaetterhenry! Well, they'll have you looking that way again."

But she was doubtful. She told the other boarders about how vigorous August had been and how he had aged. She said:

"I'll bet he's waited too long before he came, just like all those old farmers. He looks to me as if he might have had some kind of a stroke. Did you notice how kind of slow he moves? Well, sir, it's that big strong kind of men that sometimes goes all of a sudden."

She frightened Emma who had never actually noticed before how changed August was. It was hard to say what the change was, exactly. He was not thin. His face was still high-coloured. But the skin looked different; there were wrinkles; his figure was sunken, and his movements were no longer vigorous; his eye was vacant and seemed to turn slowly. The whole impression of the man was different.

Emma and the children had wondered if August would ever submit to all those tests and examinations. He had always scorned all such things. It had taken him a long while to give up, but now he had done so completely. He was

169

suddenly not the same person. He was meek.
He let Emma do things for him, turned to her.
He seemed to depend upon her. When they
went to the clinic, he let her make all the ar-
rangements. And he called her in and let her
answer many of the questions that the doctor
asked. All the time, from the doctor's careful,
non-committal manner—a new doctor, large and
calm—from something that they felt, but could
not name, they were afraid.

August had fought all these months against
having anything done for him, against "seeing
anyone." But now that it might be too late,
he was suddenly ready to do anything. He went
through all the tests without a murmur, and he
even seemed to find a relief in having his ailments
admitted to the doctor. August! He seemed
to want Emma's help and sympathy. Before,
he wouldn't even so much as admit that his
stomach was out of order, was angry with anyone
who dared to suggest it.

They had both been hoping that the doctor
would say that there must be an operation.
Since Emma had been helped by an operation, it
seemed to them that an operation would do anything. But the doctor merely said that this con-

dition could hardly be helped by that. He
wouldn't say much about it all, only murmuring
something about "blood pressure pretty high."
He was going to give August a diet, and he was
to do no physical work not to drive the car, to
be quiet and avoid excitement. August and
Emma did not say to each other what was meant,
but they knew. "High blood pressure" was a
term of terror to people in Richland, although
old Dr. Bowen laughed at the whole business and
said there was no such thing. Everyone said
that that was what had caused Mrs. Vesey's
stroke. The doctor's coolness, his temperate
statements, only soothed them for the time being.
"Stroke" was what they were both fearing. It
was the fear of all the elderly people in Richland. Time was counted from the day when
Mrs. Vesey or Grandpa Granger or Fred
Williams had had a stroke.

Emma was all the more fearful because the
doctor kept her and questioned her closely about
the time last summer when August had been overcome with the heat. She answered timidly,
half consciously trying to make it sound less
serious than it had been, for fear of that word.
But she had to ask the doctor what he thought it

171

had been. He would admit no more than that it might have been slightly on the order of a stroke. But he let her know that August's condition was serious.

August had a reaction from his meekness before the doctors. The night before they left Rochester he was discouraged. He let himself sink into bitter depths of hopelessness. He blamed the doctors. He said that if he'd known they weren't going to do any more for him than that, he wouldn't have come up here and wasted all his money. Just tell him to be careful! Any old fool, even old Doc Bowen, could have done that. He didn't need to come clear up to Minnesota to learn a thing like that. Emma tried to soothe him. She defended the doctors.

"Well, maybe there ain't anything else they could do. They said there wasn't anything to operate for. I suppose there's times when they can't. They gave you a diet."

"*Ja*, diet!" he said bitterly. "Think if I can't do anything else, then I might as well starve too, a'ready."

They admitted to the landlady that they didn't think August had got much help. It seemed to both of them that the doctors should

172

have *done* more. August declared that he
believed that stuff he'd taken last summer had
given him more help. They both thought that
if Emma's old doctor could have looked at him,
he might have done something. "If he helped
you, why couldn't he have helped me?" Their
notion of medicine was still as of some universal
panacea. August had looked to "operation"
and "Rochester" as the last resort, the final
magic independent of what he himself did.
Now it seemed that there was no panacea.

They went home silent and discouraged, fearful, hating to admit to the children and the
neighbours what had been said. They had not
sent word that they were coming. There was
no one to meet them at the little station, standing bleak in the midst of frozen winter pastures.
They went up the lonely, icy street. They had
had a discussion about the suit-case. Emma
had been afraid to have August carry it all the
way home. She had wanted to leave it in the
depot. One of the boys would be in town soon
and could get it. He had angrily refused.
Then she had said:

"Well, let me take it, then. I don't want you
to carry it. You'll hurt yourself." He picked

173

it up and went angrily on with it, she trotting over the ice at his side and urging him to let her have it.

Then they met one of their neighbours, Lew Parsons, in his car. He stopped at the corner, called, "Hello! didn't know you folks was back! Don't you want to ride home?" They climbed in thankfully. "*Ja*, I thought mister oughtn't to carry that suit-case, but he wouldn't give it up," Emma said.

Lew Parsons said, "Well, what did they do to you up there?" August said gloomily, "*Ach*, not much of anything." "Not much of anything, hey? Well, I could have told you before you went how it would be. Them places makes a big noise, but there's some stuff right down here at the drug-store that me and the missus always takes when we got anything the matter with us, and it does the business."

They went into their house. The furnace was out. The place was ice-cold. Emma worried over anything that August did, but he was determined not to let her help him start the fire. It was a bleak home-coming.

The children came in when they found that "the folks" were at home. There wasn't much

to tell them. Emma said the doctors hadn't
had much to say.

But people in town gradually knew. They
said that Mr. Kaetterhenry had "high blood
pressure," and that they'd told him he was
liable to have a stroke. One might take him off
any time, and they marvelled again over what
a big strong man he had always seemed to be.
They said that was often the way. They had
time in Richland to watch and study people, to
go minutely over and over physical symptoms,
to see what kind of people seemed to last and
what didn't.

All that winter August sat around the house,
went down occasionally for the mail. Emma
was fearful. She watched him. If she didn't
know where he was and what he was doing,
she sent Marguerite to see. People said, "He's
failed just since they come back from Rochester."
They saw how slowly he walked. His feet
dragged as he went past their houses to the post
office. He never went out to the farm any more.
He said he didn't want to go there.

They were not content with merely diet and
care. They tried other things. Another brand
of medicine, and then a treatment for "high

175

blood pressure," regardless of cause, that a doctor in "Wapsie" gave. They thought at first that it might be helping. Then they couldn't tell whether it did or not. Mrs. Cooley, who, people whispered, was "kind of a Christian Scientist or some such thing," told Emma about a man over at Wellington who claimed to give people mental healing. She wanted Emma to take August over there and have him try that. Emma was quite worked up over all the wonders of which Mrs. Cooley had told her, but August refused to go. Although, in medical matters, he was quite ready to believe in magic, it must be connected with something that he could see, a bottle or a knife. He said that this was "nothing but some more Christian Science," and that he had always considered almost equal in wickedness to Catholicism.

In the summer he seemed to be a little better. Perhaps it was because he could get out more. He mowed the lawn, although Emma didn't like to have him do it. He went downtown and stood about with the other men. The anxiety that had been hanging over them lightened a little. But there was always the fear of that day he might do a little too much.

176

The day came. There was a sale of stock out in the country, and August secretly took the car and drove out there. All of a sudden he had got tired of hanging around, and had broken loose. It happened to be one of the very hottest days of the whole summer. Emma did not know that August had gone, but she knew what it meant when she saw Carl driving up the street in their sedan. He and Dr. Brady were bringing August home.

That evening everyone in town knew of it.

"Have you heard about Mr. Kaetterhenry's stroke? *Ja*, he had a stroke this afternoon out at Gorensen's sale; ain't expected to live. Well, I guess they been kind of expecting it a long time."

The children were summoned. They drove in from the country. It had been a severe stroke. Their father might not live through the night. In all their hearts was the hope that he would not "live to be like grandma."

Several times they thought that he was dying. They went into the bedroom where he lay unconscious. But he was a vigorous man, and it took the thing a long time to kill him. He lived for three days. The children had to go back to

177

their farms, and only Roy and Elva were there when he had another stroke and died.

"August Kaetterhenry's dead! He died at three o'clock." That was what everyone in Richland was saying now. He had never regained consciousness. They all said again how strange it seemed. What a strong man he had seemed to be when he first moved to town— had looked as if he would live for years! They remembered how he had helped to build his new house. They said what a pity that he had lived so few years to enjoy it. Now everyone was wondering where and when the funeral would be. The Kaetterhenrys were such Methodists, probably it would be in the church.

Funerals were still public events in Richland. This one was expected to be large. A great many people came in from the country. Towns-people turned out, although they hadn't known August very well, to see what kind of service it would be and who was there. All the pews were filled as Tom Peters, who was studying with the local undertaker, led one family after another to their places in a creaking silence. They wanted to hear what the Methodist quartet, Dr. Brady, Herb Carter, Willie Stille, and Mr. Rush, would sing. Most of all, they wanted to see "who had come from away." They whispered, "My, he must have had a lot of relations!" "Well, some of these are hers."

The five front rows at the side were reserved for the mourners. There were all the children and the children-in-law and the grandchildren. Grandpa Stille, of course, couldn't get in, although he had wanted to come, had sighed and mourned over "the young folks going." Herman and Mollie Klaus were there. There were five families of Stilles Those whom people really wanted to see were "his folks," who had come from Turkey Creek. Sophie Klaus and her husband, Heinie and Ferdinand Kaetterhenry and their wives. Mina had come. She was a fat, toothless old widow now. She had always cared the most for August, although he had not done much for her. She wore a little scrap of cheap black veiling on her ancient summer hat. The two brothers were heavier men than August, more like the old man Kaetterhenry.

There was a long procession of cars that went out to the cemetery. Most of them were from the country. All the children and all the relatives from Turkey Creek, and a good many of the other country people from the Richland neighbourhood. It pleased the Turkey Creek relatives to see how many. August had been the most successful brother, and Richland was more metropolitan than Turkey Creek.

They drove down the hard, brown, dusty road, slowly, stopping so that the cars wouldn't bump into one another. They went through the big iron gate of the cemetery, which was open to-day. The relatives looked around and whispered, "Oh, that's where his lot is. It's in a nice spot." August had bought the lot when he moved to town. It was over in the newer part of the cemetery, near a large evergreen.

The summer wind stirred in the unaccustomed black veils of the women as they stood about the grave. "Must be a country funeral," people driving past said when they saw all the waiting cars and the solemn, stolid group of people there.

The children had to drive home to do the chores. But August's sister Sophie and the Ferdinand Kaetterhenrys were going to spend the night with Emma, so that she and Marguerite wouldn't be alone. The Henry and the Willie Stilles came over in the evening.

They talked about August, in voices slightly hushed, but more natural now that it was all over. They said how nice the funeral had been, how many had driven in from the country. They talked about the sermon. "This good brother who has gone before us," the minister had said. That was right. They said what a good church-member, how faithful, August had always been! Ferdinand said he remembered when he and August had "gone forward" at one of the old Turkey Creek camp-meetings. August had been faithful to his pledge. The minister had said what a good citizen and good farmer August had been. They said that that was true. Sophie and Ferdinand were proud of how much August had been able to accumulate when they remembered the old days in the cabin down on Turkey Creek. They said he had worked hard for all he had got. He had deserved it. The only pity was that he hadn't lived to get more enjoyment out of it.

Then they talked over the details of his illness. They said how quickly he had seemed to fail when he once started. It didn't seem any time since he was over at Turkey Creek the last time and had helped Heinie with the haying.

181

Emma cried a little. It seemed to her that August had had to work so hard, and then after he moved to town he hadn't got much out of all his work. They gave her vague consolations: "Well, we don't understand why he should have been taken this way, but, then, there's some reason." But they thought as she did. It didn't seem right that Herman Klaus, for instance, was still living, as well and happy as ever, and August was gone. They had thought of that when they had looked at Herman at the funeral.

There was consolation and pride in the column of close print in the Richland *Banner* on Thursday. Emma ordered extra copies.

"ESTEEMED RESIDENT PASSES"

And below, in smaller type:

"RETIRED FARMER ANSWERS SUMMONS."

August's life seemed different to her, more important, as she read it there, as if she had been reading about a stranger.

"On Sunday last the grim Reaper called from our midst an esteemed citizen, Mr. August Kaetterhenry.

182

Obituary

August Ernst Kaetterhenry was born on a farm near Turkey Creek, Iowa, on September 10, 1859. He was the fifth son of Casper and Luisa Kaetterhenry, who were natives of Pommern, Germany."

She read, as if she had never known it before, how August had had "such education as the schools of that day afforded," how he had "left his native township and come to Richland Township to seek his fortune, working for a time on the farm of the late Henry Baumgartner, well-known Richland Township farmer." Then how "he was united in marriage with Emma Stille, daughter of Wilhelm, now known as Grandpa Stille, and to them six children were born, all of whom survive." How he had acquired the farm, how he had made it into one of the best improved farms in Richland Township, "where the deceased's son, Carl Kaetterhenry, is now operating the farm on the principles taught him by his father. . . . Mr. Kaetterhenry was known to all his neighbours as a conscientious farmer and an honest, upright man. He united with the Methodist denomination when a young man, and was all his life one of its most faithful members and one whose loss will be felt by the church and community. . . .

183

Mr. Kaetterhenry is survived by his sorrowing widow, Mrs. Emma Kaetterhenry, and by his children Frank, Mrs. Joe Fields, Mrs. Roy Robbins, Carl, John, and Marguerite and by numerous grandchildren. Also by his sisters Mrs. Ed Klaus and Mrs. Mina Nisson and brothers Henry and Ferdinand Kaetterhenry, all of Turkey Creek."

She had never seen all their names in print before. "Esteemed resident," "retired farmer" —it sounded like someone else than August.

Emma cut these columns out from several papers and folded the strips in the old "doctor-book" that lay on the doily on the bottom shelf of the bookcase behind the glass door.

III: *The Estate*

THEN there was all the settling-up of the estate to be done.

August had never let Emma know anything of business affairs. Of late years he had permitted her to do a small amount of the buying, but he had never thought of letting her handle anything that was not directly connected with the household. He had bought the meat, subscribed for the papers, planned the garden, managed everything. Now, suddenly, she had to see to all these things.

It worried her at first. Even a little thing like sending the "card of thanks" that must be inserted in the next issue of the *Banner:*

"WE, the undersigned, wish to thank our friends and neighbours for their kindness to us during the illness and death of our husband and father and for the beautiful flowers.

"(Signed) MRS. EMMA KAETTERHENRY.
"THE CHILDREN."

Country People

There was one of these cards in every issue of the *Banner*, and Emma always read them conscientiously, but still she did not know how to go about it to have her own put there. She made Johnnie write it for her and take it down to the *Banner* office.

She hadn't been used to getting the mail. She didn't know whether to keep on subscribing for the farm journal or not. She "hated to let it go," since August had taken it so long. She could not conceive of subscribing instead for a household magazine for herself. That seemed too audacious. She had scarcely been inside the bank. She had no idea how to make out a cheque, and was afraid of her cheque-book. She employed devices for getting out of going to the bank, such as making out a cheque to Johnnie under his directions and having him cash it, and keeping the money that came in to her from this and that. Although Johnnie explained the cheque-book to her, she said that she would never know from that how much money she had, not unless her money was somewhere where she could see it and "keep track of it." She was afraid to draw a cent. She liked to keep silver and odd change in an old tea-pot in the cupboard, as she had kept the egg money. There was the worry over what to do with the car. She would never use it. She hated to have it "sitting in the garage." Some of these auto thieves might steal it.

There were all the little worries, too, that immediately followed August's death. For a time she was "pestered" by catalogues and visits from monument men from Dubuque and Rapids City. One of the salesmen, a slick young fellow with bright grey eyes set too close together, upset her dreadfully by wanting her to order a large monument and two markers with "Father" and "Mother," promising her a reduction if she would get all three. Emma said, "It would make me think I was dead a'ready." The children said that she needn't order the things, but Emma told them that she didn't see how else she was ever going to get rid of that fellow. She even got a sample copy of the old-fashioned black memorial cards with a verse and the name in gold, "Mr. August Kaetterhenry." She wondered how those people had known that August was dead, and how they had got his name. She remembered that they had had cards like that when her oldest sister Bertha had died,

187

but they were so "gloomy-looking" that she was glad the children didn't want her to get them now.

People were interested to hear whether August had left a will. There would be a muddle if he hadn't. Emma said, "*Ach*, I don't think pa ever made a will." But he had made one, it seemed, when he had moved into town, although he hadn't told them anything about it. The lawyer, E. P. Bland, read it to all of them. Emma had never known before "what they had." She did not understand very well now. She had thought that Frank owned the farm where he lived, but it seemed that August had still been the owner of it. Now both the farms were hers. She was to have some rent from both of them. There was the stock in the bank, which was divided among the family, and a little piece of land in Montana that no one had known that August had, and that went to the children. Emma had the house and lot in town. She was "pretty well fixed." August had accumulated more than Emma had thought; not so much as certain people in town had predicted, who always said of other people, "Aw, he's got more tucked away than anybody knows about." Of course

188

Emma would have the taxes and insurance and repairs, things she had never thought of before.

The children wanted to sell that Montana land at once and get what they could out of it. They had always been a little afraid of their father. Even after he had left the farm and moved to town, the thought of him had checked them. Now they began to blossom out a little, to get things, to think of themselves as really adult.

Frank wouldn't do much differently than he had been doing. He was a settled young-old farmer, short and small and very quiet, a good steady worker, but one who was not likely to get ahead very far. He and Lottie had a horde of children, and they were one of those families who are always having accidents, sickness, and doctor's bills. Frank was caught in the gasolene engine and just missed being killed or mangled. Lottie, big sturdy woman that she was, had had several operations performed by her brother-in-law, a doctor in Bishop. There was one thing after another the matter with the children. Their farm was an untidy place, much like their uncle Herman's.

Carl would do better. He was going to make

as good a farmer as his father. Better, some
people thought. While he might not be able to
keep at it quite so doggedly, might not be quite
so saving, he was more ready to try things, less
stubborn and set in his ways. He was just as
particular about the buildings and machinery as
August had been. His wife, Clara, was a
hustler. She had nearly a thousand chickens,
and was making money with them. Her canned
goods took prizes at the Farmers' Institute in the
armoury building in "Wapsie." Carl and Clara
worked hard, but they "went," too. They were
going to have some fun as they went along.
They had no fear of poverty in their old age.

The farm looked very different now. Carl
had had the house "pebble-dashed." August's
name was gone from the barn now, which was
painted a new shining white.

Mary, in a way, scarcely belonged to the
family any more; she and Joe lived so far
away, or it seemed far away. They were
part of the Adams Grove neighbourhood now,
and did their trading in Bishop. Joe's farm
was in the timber country there. There were
some limestone cliffs and a little glen on the edge
of their own land. The whole country was

different from that around Richland. Not just like the Turkey Creek country, but hilly and backwoodsy and queer.

(Mary and Joe seemed to be happy together.) Mary had never had much but hard work out of life, except for those few years when she had been a mysterious invalid. She had two children of her own besides the other four. There was no more time for books now than she had ever had, but she found an outlet in the neighbourhood church, where she taught a large Sunday-school class and worked with the young people. She went with them to Epworth League conventions, and she was famed for having the best papers in the missionary society. Sunday school was the only glimpse of anything besides "practical work" that Mary had ever known.

Elva and Roy were talking now of moving to Oklahoma. Roy had a cousin who had an interest in some oil-wells out there, and Roy was wild to go, "quit this farming."

Johnnie was turning out better now. He bought out the Beal brothers in the garage, and he took the little house near his mother's where Nannie Frost had lived. The garage was on a highway and did a good business. But it

191

worried Emma that it kept Johnnie so busy all
the time. He was up until all hours of the
night. He was a good mechanic. The fact that
he was dealing with things that would go, his
sight of passing travel, eased his restlessness.
He was less nervous now. But he had never
been the same boy since the war. It seemed to
have affected Johnnie and Carl in opposite ways.

Johnnie was tremendously fond of Junior, but
otherwise he was not very happy at home. He
had no illusions about Bernice. He knew that
she was a fool. She was shiftless, and there were
frequent ructions with his mother-in-law. He
seemed to enjoy being near his mother, although
he seldom went in and talked to her. He
brought home the mail for her and cashed cheques
and saw about the insurance. She was better
satisfied when she thought of him now; but
it worried her that Johnnie seemed to care
nothing for the church. She tried, timidly and
anxiously, to get him to go. He usually said
that he couldn't get away from the garage, but
once he told her, "No, mamma, I'm all through
with that. It don't mean anything to me."
She thought that perhaps it came from having a
business that ran on Sunday, and that grandpa

had been right: this Sunday travel was going to ruin the country. That wild streak in Johnnie that had troubled them for a while seemed to be wearing off, but there was a kind of bitterness that she couldn't understand. She thought Johnnie looked older than Carl. He was so thin! And his sunburned skin, his fair hair, his oil-stained khaki overalls seemed all of a colour —the colour of the dust on the highway that followed the wheels of the cars going endlessly past the garage.

Marguerite had finished the high school now. Emma would have liked to have her stay at home for company, but Marguerite wanted to go and take a business course in Rapids City. Half the youth of Richland were going to business college now, either in Rapids City or Dubuque, and Marguerite had to go, too. She wanted to earn money of her own, so that she could buy the kind of clothes she liked. She wanted to be in a larger town.

All of the children lived better than their parents had done, unless it was Mary. They came into town often, and they thought nothing of driving to Dubuque for a day. They had all given elaborate names to their children, which
193

sounded absurd with the old German surnames:
Maxine, Velda, Delight, Gwendolyn, Eugene,
Dwayne.

Not long after August's death, Emma went
out to Mollie's to see her father. Carl took her
out and was to call for her. She hadn't been
there for months. Grandpa Stille was over
ninety now. Who could tell how much longer
he might be there?

It was a sunny September day. The willows
along the edge of Herman's farm sprinkled
narrow, shiny, yellow leaves over the drive
where they turned in, which had a patch of
smooth, leathery, brownish-black mud, with
cracks across it. The dingy house and the
scraggly grove had a kind of beauty to-day in the
sunshine and the burning blue sky.

She found grandpa in his room on the west of
the house, the window looking out on the willow
grove. Mollie took her in to him, went up, and
shouted:

"Pa, *sieh wer hier ist!*"

He peered forward.

"*Ach, ja, ja, ja—Emma ist's? Ja, so!*" He
put out a hand that trembled slightly.

He was thinner, bonier than ever, his hair only

194

a few long silver wisps under an old skull-cap,
his mouth sunken in under his beard. His deep-
set brown eyes still had life in them. Despite
the age and the dinginess, those dark quilts that
she knew so well on the billowing feather-bed,
the bare floor painted a dark red, there was a
beauty that she felt in the old room to-day, with
the September sunlight slanting in through the
window and a rustling sound from the willow
grove.

Mollie and Herman had told her that the old
man seldom talked to them now. He seemed to
be somewhere in a place of his own. Yet his
mind, when he did talk, was as clear as ever.
Now that the dreadful war was over, he had
gone back to his dreams. He came back with
an effort, repeated her name, sighed over the
death of August *so jung*, but declared that there
was no great sorrow in dying; roused to ask her
why *die kleine Marguerite* never came out to see
her old grandpa. They talked in German. He
answered her when she told him where Marguerite was now and what the boys were doing, of
August's death. He was kind, and held her
hand as she talked, looked at her with affection
in his thin old face, told her that she was a good

195

girl. He mourned that she should have lost her husband. But when she left him he seemed to go back at once into that reverie in which he lived now, broken only by occasional mutterings, as in the old days. But they were peaceful mutterings now.

She stayed awhile with Mollie. They talked about their father. Emma said:

"Grandpa seems to be real content."

"*Ach, ja,*" Mollie said easily, "he's always happy."

"*Ja,* but what does he do in there alone all day? I should think he'd get awful' lonesome."

"No, he don't get lonesome. *Ach,* I don't know what he does. He always seems to have plenty to think about. He used to read, but that he can't do any more."

"I hate to see him sit alone like that."

"*Ach,* he's all right."

What was he doing, thinking? Mollie said that sometimes they heard him singing old German hymns, so old that she didn't know them. He wanted nothing but his tobacco, his meals, wood for his stove in winter.

Mollie had gone to the kitchen for some eggs that she was going to give Emma to take home.

Emma heard the old man, in his room, praying.
She had forgotten how he used to do that, so that
it startled her for a moment. The German
words, guttural, rich, with long pauses between,
had a sound that was unearthly and yet fitting
in the still, sunlit country air. She looked into
his room. He sat in the old wooden rocker.
His deep eyes had a withdrawn, mystic look.
He did not notice her. Mollie said:

"*Ja*, we often hear him doing that."

Emma thought about it as Carl was driving
her home between the September fields of dusty
gold in the late afternoon. She could still hear
those faint, far-apart, devout German words.
August had always said that if her father had
been more of a farmer and less of a preacher, he'd
be better off to-day. August had despised him
in a dispassionate way. But the old man had
had something, she hardly knew what, that had
lasted him when his work was over.

"He's got something to think about," she
thought.

It was that something, she could not name it,
which she had missed all her married life.

She remembered the pathos of August, coming
in from the farm and saying bitterly that every-

thing had to go Carl's way now; of him sitting about the house, trying to look at the farm journal, not knowing what to do with himself. Her father, what a frail man he had been when he had first come to live with them years ago! And here he was living still, contented with the little that he had, and well, and August was the one who was gone.

IV: *Mrs. Emma Kaetterhenry*

RETIRED farmers, widows, spinsters—these
made up most of the little town of Richland. Emma was one of the widows
now—widows living alone on small independent
incomes, on the rents from farms, or helped by
their children.

Marguerite was in Rapids City now. Women
in Richland said disapprovingly that she ought
to have stayed with her mother, but they were
appeased by hearing that Marguerite was making
twenty-two dollars a week as a stenographer.
And they heard that she was engaged to that
young fellow who sometimes came home with
her, although she didn't seem to be marrying him.

She came home over Sunday sometimes. She
brought her "friend," a slim, glossy-haired young
man who was employed in an office in Rapids
City, and who had bought a second-hand car in
which they drove to Richland. They drove
down on Sunday morning, and after dinner they

either sat talking in low, meaning voices while
Emma dozed—"You didn't? Oh, you did, too.
How do *I* know? Sure I know!"—or drove out
to Carl's. Emma told Marguerite that she
ought to stop and see grandpa; but when they
came back, and she asked them about it, Marguerite said, "Oh, we didn't get over there this
time." Emma did not know whether these two
were engaged or not.

Marguerite had converted herself into a very
urban young lady. Her chief business in staying in Rapids City was to watch the proper
length of skirts and waists and to have everything right. She was tall, still thin, and wore
her clothes well. The only thing about her looks
that really worried her was that her hair was too
fuzzy to take a wave well. She and another
girl were doing their own cooking in light-
housekeeping rooms, and what she saved on food
she spent on clothes. Emma thought it was
dreadful when she saw what Marguerite was
wearing out to Carl's, "just out in the country"
—those sheer dresses and light, high-heeled
slippers and silk stockings. But she did nothing
more than murmur:

Mrs. Emma Kaetterhenry

"Is that what you're going to wear out there? Won't you spoil it?"

Marguerite was a real Kaetterhenry however. At home she had done none of the work, but now that she had a job, although the interest of her life was in clothes, she did her work well and disdained the slipshod ways of other stenographers. She was cool, hard, scrupulous, level-headed, a good worker. She seemed to be a nice, capable girl, people in Richland had decided, although she wasn't much comfort to her mother.

Even if she was alone, there were still claims upon Emma. There was the aid society, of which she was now one of the chief supports. She still worked in the kitchen at church suppers. She was sent for when there was sickness in the country. She was often called upon to keep the grandchildren while Carl and Clara, or Elva and Roy, drove to Dubuque. Some of the little ones stayed with her while the others were sick with measles or whooping-cough or scarlet fever. She often had Junior with her. Bernice was "always on the go," or fancied that she had something the matter with her. "Ma"— "grandma" they were beginning to call her—was still the stand-by of all the children, and "grandma's house" was the place where they all expected to go when they went to town.

But in a way she was knowing leisure for the first time in her life. She did not feel the responsibility that she had felt when things were dependent upon her alone. She always had plenty of time to herself. She was doing what she pleased in ways that she had never done before. She had friends outside her home, elderly ladies like herself, with whom she spent pleasant, gossipy afternoons, as she hadn't done while August was living. Her personality, smothered and silent for many years, was blossoming out, very faintly and timidly, but a little, enough to shed a kind of light of content and freedom over this quiet end of life. She might be lonely later on, but she was not now. She was a Stille, not a Kaetterhenry. That showed now. She could be happy pottering about on her own devices. The children said ma got along better alone than they'd been afraid she would.

She had gradually got used to the fact that money was her own, that there was no one but herself to say what she should spend and what she shouldn't. She did not say much about it, but not even her children realized what a wonder and pleasure it was to her to have a little money in her own hands. She still felt timid and out of place when she went into the bank. She made the boys do it for her. She was still very cautious about what she spent, could not overcome the lifelong habit of hoarding and thinking about the future. It seemed wicked to her to spend more than a very little on herself, she had had the self-effacement of mother and wife so ground into her. But when she admired a piece of goods in the store window, she could think, "Well, I can have it if I want it." She needn't ask anybody.

She could enjoy buying small presents for the grandchildren, getting cloth to make up for them, sending dollar bills in letters to Marguerite so that she could get herself something she wanted. She gave generously when she was solicited for the church, and people said, "I guess it was him that was the close one more than she. She gives real freely." She no longer had to turn away agents who came to the house selling things that she didn't want, something that had always given her tender and sentimental heart a guilty

203

feeling. She said "they might need it; you could never be sure." She'd rather take the chance and not send anyone away. She had never subscribed for the household magazine that she wanted, thinking three dollars a year almost too sinful a waste for reading-matter; but she had a little magazine at which she never looked, having given her subscription to a young Armenian—"a young foreigner," she called him —who had asked her to "vote for him" by giving him a subscription. The youth who got the most of these "votes" would be elected by the magazine company for a year at college. She never heard whether her young foreigner had been elected.

Emma even talked of taking a trip some time out to Nebraska to see her brother Ed. But just as soon as the children began to press her to go, she would begin to make excuses. She did not quite have the courage to make a trip, or decide on one, by herself. If they had gone while pa was still alive, then that would have been different.

The children could hardly believe their Aunt Mollie when she told them that as a girl their mother had "liked to go." Now it was hard for them to get ma even to drive to Dubuque with

them. She only told them mildly, ach, she had
forgotten how, she'd stayed at home so much.
It was something that she had looked forward to
when they were working so hard on the farm,
that when they "once had something" and "got
to town," she could go again as much as she
pleased. She did not tell the children now how
timid she felt about starting out anywhere, how
she "seemed better off at home."

They could not believe, either, that she had
been a giggler, as Mollie said. There was a
picture of Emma and Mollie in the album, taken
in the same dresses and hats that they had worn
to the Richland Grove Fourth of July celebration, the first place where Emma had gone
with August. The children laughed over Aunt
Mollie's spit-curls, and said that she needn't
talk; and their mother's hat with a ridiculous
feather, the attitude of the two girls sitting there
displaying their finery. The children said,
"Don't you talk to us!" But they couldn't
really believe that their quiet, shy mother had
been as she looked in that photograph.

But she did go a little, more than she had been
doing. She never missed church, of course. She
went to the "aids" and the missionary-meetings.

Country People

She got Mrs. Henry Stille to stop for her and went to the Social Circle Club. She didn't mind going to places so much if she had someone to go with her. She enjoyed entertaining the club more now than when she had felt that it was bothering August. He had grumbled about "What do all those women want to sit around and talk for? Better go home and look after their houses." She felt more free to serve what refreshments she pleased.

She looked better than she had for years, a plump, shapeless, elderly woman, with grey hair a little curling; spectacles—good ones now, with light, narrow shell rims; she had got them "up at Rochester"—and mild, soft, faded brown eyes. She was dowdy and countrified, but wore clothes of lasting materials, always having one good silk dress, and letting Marguerite persuade her to buy a new spring hat instead of wearing her old one again.

She still got up early every morning. Not so early as when August was living, however. Then they were awake at four, as they had been in the country. Now she lay abed sometimes until after six o'clock. That gave her a scared, delicious, audacious feeling. She liked to work in the garden in the early morning. She enjoyed having time for flowers. She had always had a few on the farm, but couldn't take care of them. They were food for her sense of beauty. Now she chose the seeds herself. She planted moss roses near the house and had Johnnie put up a trellis, shocked that he did it on Sunday. She liked to be out there planting in the spring. She put on an ancient black calico wrapper, a sunbonnet, a black, padded, sleeveless jacket, and some old shoes of August's, and went out in the yard. It was silent and sunny, no sound but an occasional car on the road, a rooster crowing, sometimes the noise of Junior's little kiddy-car on the cement walk. She liked the feel of the cool spring earth, sun-warmed on the surface, black and moist and chill underneath, as she patted it over the tiny dry seeds. She talked to Junior, said, "Dig over there in the corner, Junie, if you have to dig too, then"; but her mind was far away from him, in some wordless place of mysterious content.

She ate most of her meals alone at the little table in the kitchen. That was what she minded most of living alone—the meals. Carl and Clara had made her promise that she would cook herself real meals and not just take to lunching, as many women did when they had no men to cook for. She obeyed them pretty well, although sometimes she said, *"Ach,* just for myself!" She took great pains with her housework, although she worked slowly since there was no reason to hurry. There was a kind of mystery and contentment, too, in moving about the quiet, bright house as she worked. She wanted to keep the floors as shining as when the house was new. It worried her, although she did not say so, to have the grandchildren "get things around." After they had gone, she went about picking things up after them. She had never had time for that on the farm.

In the afternoon she often had to take care of Junior for Bernice. He was her favourite, although she would not say so, of all the grandchildren, just as Johnnie had secretly been her favourite of the children. Junior didn't seem to have suffered from the shortcomings of his mother. He was one of the sturdiest babies in town, one of whom women said lovingly, "That dear little Junior Kaetterhenry!" and men. "Ain't he a buster, though!" His fat, white cheeks and his brown eyes and his engaging smile, the fact that he had won second place in the baby-show in "Wapsie," consoled his grandmother for the fact that Johnnie had made a poor marriage, and that he didn't go to church or "believe." It seemed that the Lord must not be angry with Johnnie, since he had given him Junior. She baked cookies so that she would have some for Junior—"gran'ma's cookies," he called them—and had bought some little celluloid animals at the ten-cent store in Dubuque. He followed her about the house and asked questions, and shrieked "Daddy!" when any man went past in an automobile. And yet she felt it a kind of strain to have him there. She loved him, but she felt a kind of relief when Bernice came flouncing in to get him and take him home.

She did more fancy work now. She liked to make little clothes for the grandchildren, and tried to be very impartial with them. Marguerite picked out "cute patterns" for her in Rapids City. These little youngest Kaetterhenrys dressed very differently than her children had done. She made little bright-coloured chambray frocks, with apples and morning-glories in appliqué.

She had to care for the lot in the cemetery.

She got Johnnie to drive her out there. She said that she didn't mind walking back, and usually there was someone coming along in a car who would take her as far as town. The monument was up now, a large, square, polished grey stone, with "KAETTERHENRY" carved upon it; below that:

"AUGUST ERNST
1859–1922"

and below that a space. But she had not bought her own marker. Johnnie had got rid of the monument man for her. She had had a photograph taken of the lot when the stone was put up, and she cherished that.

She kept a vase on August's grave, which she filled with flowers in the summer, although the bunches of sweet-peas and cosmos frequently withered before she could get out with a fresh bouquet. She had had a small bridal-wreath bush set out in a corner of the lot. This summer she was going to have a border of that little pink love-in-a-mist around the grave. She wanted her lot to look as well as any in the cemetery.

The Richland cemetery was in a high, sunny

spot. She was not unhappy as she went about there, filling the vase, moving slowly down the narrow path through the thick grass to the small iron gate.

She told the children that she did not lack for company. Another elderly widow who had been a farmer's wife, Mrs. Wall, lived on the next street in a large, square house painted pale blue. Emma called for Mrs. Wall, and they went to the prayer-meeting and the evening church-service together, and to the missionary-meeting and the "aid." It "made it nice for both of them," people said.

Mrs. Wall came over sometimes in the evening. They sat together, sometimes in the front room, or "just out in the kitchen." Mrs. Wall knew more of what was going on than Emma did, although she said that she didn't hear so much now that she didn't have a man coming home from town. They talked over illnesses and approaching weddings and of those whom they had seen going past their houses that day. Emma told Mrs. Wall about her operation, and Mrs. Wall told her about those of sisters and sisters-in-law and brothers. They talked about the birth of children and grandchildren. Each one found a consolation in detailing to the other the last illness and death of her husband—all the symptoms from week to week, the death, the laying-out, the funeral, in hushed, confiding voices, shaking their heads and murmuring, "Yes, oh, it must have been terrible. I know what that is." They sat in the twilight together, sympathizing and condoling and narrating. Emma said it helped her to have someone to tell these things to. She would not have told them to the children.

The two women talked of religion together, of what they thought heaven was going to be like, of the way that they thought God looked at things. Emma had no such mystic fervour as her old father, but the hymns, the prayers, the familiar words, were an emotional satisfaction. They comforted her.

They talked of their troubles, said of them that such things were hard to bear; they didn't always see why they must be—Johnnie's getting such a poor wife and turning away from the church, Grandma Stille's helplessness, Mr. Wall's sufferings from cancer. These women had both worked hard. Now they were getting old, and many things had not turned out as they had thought they would.

Mrs. Wall sometimes said:

"Well, we've all had our troubles. All had things to go through. Well, I say we ought to be thankful that we've got good homes, and children to look after us if we need it; that we don't have to be sent to the poorhouse like that poor old woman in Bishop the other day. Did you hear about that?"

Emma said:

"*Ja*, that's true, too."

THE END